Lunch Special

Lunch Special

Ron Johnson

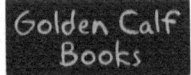

Golden Calf Books

Published by Golden Calf Books

ISBN 978-0-692-17990-1

Cover Art Concept: Ron Johnson
Cover Art Designer: Pintado www.pintado.weebly.com

Discuss the book with other readers and stay updated on future releases at the *Lunch Special* Facebook page: facebook.com/lunchspecialbook/

Typesetting services by BOOKOW.COM

For my little boy

Preface

For the best experience, the short stories in *Lunch Special* should be read through in one sitting.

-RJ

"Everybody gotta die sometime, Red."

—Sgt Barnes, *Platoon*

Contents

For Dog and Country

"Bobby, come on dude I gotta go to work."

"Gimme a minute, I'm looking for something," Bobby thinks to himself. Bobby circles the spot, then circles back around the other way.

Dave sighs and checks his watch.

Bobby shoves his long nose down through the grass and pauses in deep thought. "Nope that ain't it," he thinks before circling back once again.

"Bobby hurry up, we got places to be," Dave says, exasperation tinting his voice.

"Just ten more sec—" Bobby suddenly stops circling. He takes two determined steps forward, scrunches up his back and hovers over the target.

Dave gives Bobby some slack in the leash and expands a poop bag as Bobby takes his morning dump.

"Bullseye," Bobby grins to himself. "I could hit this mark all day long."

Bobby squeezes out the rest of last night's dinner from his long gray body. For a twenty-pound mutt, he sure shits a lot.

Bobby walks away from his pile to sniff the surrounding turf while Dave reaches down with a bagged hand to grab his poop. Bobby finds a soily patch in the grass and begins to moonwalk. Dirt flies from Bobby's feet towards Dave, who turns a shoulder to shield his face. As Bobby continues kicking up dirt, Dave finishes his bagging duty and stands up. Bobby looks up at him.

Dave smiles, "You ready bud?"

Bobby wags his tail.

* * *

Meet Army veteran Dave Sims, the 34-year-old owner/operator of *Eleven-Bravo Pest Exterminators*. Dave spends a lot of time in the Middle East by way of nightmares—terrible dreams of weapon jams, empty magazines, bearded corpses. Sometimes the corpses speak to him.

Bobby, a nine-year-old mixed-race canine, used to have nightmares. Visions of leather belts snapping his rump and poop being shoved into his snout holes. One recurring dream featured Bobby spinning in a circle with his paws stretched to the corners as some asshole kid swung him by his tail. Bobby should have lunged for the kid's balls once he hit the ground but Bobby's a lover, not a fighter, and he hasn't had a nightmare in years since meeting his pal Dave at the city pound.

Bobby's never had a better friend. Neither has Dave.

A smart man knows to never get between a man and his dog. Alas, not all men are smart.

* * *

Jake Holm is urgently sifting through two-liters and aluminum cans on the cluttered motel nightstand. "Where's the fucking Mountain Dew, Emily?"

"In the bathroom!" Emily yells from under the bed sheets, a mere three feet away from Jake.

"Why's it in the bathroom when it's supposed to be on the nightstand?"

"Because I was thirsty in the bathroom Jake, stop fucking giving me shit about the Mountain Dew!" Emily crawls around under the sheets, frantically searching for something.

Jake begins organizing items on the cluttered nightstand. Nearly every square inch is occupied by a pill bottle, aluminum can or plastic two-liter. Cigarette ash colors in what remains.

Jake changes topics. "Did you find it yet?"

Emily crawls to the foot of the bed, then slides down to the floor with a sheet-muffled grunt. Jake's focused tightly on the cluttered nightstand, rotating every container so the labels face the same direction. Emily struggles her way out from under the sheets. Standing proud, she holds up a tiny Ziploc bag of orange-white powder and flashes a gummy smile at Jake.

"I found it."

Jake's eyes flash at the bag. He reaches for it.

"Hold on," Emily says coyly as she pulls the bag backwards against her flat chest. Emily Masters, 29-years-old and barely a hundred pounds, has a body like a garter snake and she's not afraid to use it. She grabs the bottom of her knee-length t-shirt, an extra-large NASCAR rag dotted with burn holes, and lifts it up to show Jake what's underneath—dingy white panties and nothing else.

Jake's attention halves between the bag and his girl. Emily turns around to show him her backside.

"Does this look good baby?" Emily rocks her bony hips in a circle to entice Jake. Every part of Emily looks like it needs a good scrubbing.

Jake grabs Emily by the waist and lifts her off her feet. She moans in ecstasy as he carries her over to the bathroom vanity and plants her on the only place not occupied by junk: the sink basin.

Emily cringes as her dingy underwear soaks up cold water from the leaky faucet. Dirty towels and fast-food wrappers fly to the floor as Jake clears away a small spot on the vanity. He grabs the meth baggie from Emily as she arches her back uncomfortably in the basin and reaches underneath her. She pulls out a thick pack of peppermint chewing gum—the basin wasn't junk-free after all.

Jake quickly readies two lines on the vanity counter as Emily unwraps a stick of gum and sticks it in her mouth. He snorts a line as Emily watches from her basin perch.

"Ummph!" Jake grunts as he unconsciously scratches his shaved scalp.

Emily smacks her gum through smiling lips.

"Get yours baby," Jake says.

Emily reaches her feet towards the floor and clambers out of the sink. She grabs Jake's crotch before leaning over the vanity for her line. A used stick of gum, wadded up in its original foil wrapper, sticks to her sink-soaked panties.

* * *

"Hola mijo!"

Little Bobby loves the attention. Ms Lupe always speaks so sweetly to him and he especially loves the kisses she gives. Sure, she'll end up sticking her finger up his butt in the shower, but that's a small price to pay for those sugary kisses she plants right on his lips. Or more precisely, his snout—dogs don't really have lips.

"Is you gonna be a good boy today?"

Bobby wags his long mutt tail and smiles—he knows what's coming.

Lupe Menjivar loves dogs. Even though the pay is shit at Ruff Company Cut & Chew, she still enjoys her groomer job. Where else could she go to meet so many handsome dogs, day in and day out? She tried the local animal shelter but left after being vomited on by a Havanese named Jerry with a nasty case of kennel cough. She'd love to have dogs of her own but unfortunately that's not in the cards for Lupe; her Mexican landlord won't allow it because he's a Salvadoran-hating *cabron*.

"Okay mijo you stand there nice for me and I give you the kiss."

Bobby's entire rump sways side-to-side, his long body nearly bending in half with each sway. "Bring it on Ms Lupe, I'm ready for it," he thinks.

Lupe leans in and smacks a kiss right on the tip of Bobby's chinless mouth. Bobby licks her mouth to return the favor.

"Aye Bobby whatchu do funny dog!" Lupe knew the tongue was coming but took it anyways. As a single woman, dog tongue is better than no tongue at all.

"Okay mijo turn around so I shave your culo."

Bobby knows what he's supposed to do but he isn't quite sure how to make the turn on the narrow grooming table. He feints left, then right, before finally bringing his paws together indecisively.

"I help you boy," Lupe says as she grabs Bobby's torso and spins him around. "Ms Lupe always help my little chavalito."

Lupe grabs the hair clippers and clicks them on with a thunk.

Bobby looks at the clock as Lupe shaves down his buttcheeks. It's 10am—almost nap time.

Lupe navigates the clippers towards Bobby's inner thighs. He raises a leg to give her better access. She can tell that Bobby's daddy, a tall, handsome *huero* named Mr Sims, takes good care of him, because his hair isn't matted and he doesn't have fleas.

Bobby stares at Ms Lupe's tits, watching her udders jiggle while she zooms up one side of him and down the other. As she zips along his lengthy back, Bobby stuffs his snout against her blouse and takes a good long sniff. He knew it—Ms Lupe's tits smell like roses.

Lupe finishes with Bobby's haircut and places him in a cage to await shampoo and style. "Okay Bobby, you sleep and I come back for you."

"I'll be waiting for you baby," Bobby thinks to himself. "I'm gonna get my hump on after our shower."

Lupe opens the cage of a big English Sheepdog named Chappy and strolls him on over to her grooming station. At nearly three feet tall, big Chappy won't be needin' the table for his hair cut. She stoops down and looks him square in the eyes.

"Hola mijo!"

Chappy purses his lips.

* * *

Jake sits on the bed and aggressively works his phone. Dirty fingernails tap against the phone's glass as he types, enlarges, navigates, and swipes the screen. He repeats the process, again and again. Five minutes quickly become ten as Jake clacks away on his phone. Finally, he stops. Jake smiles deviously.

* * *

"This Mountain Dew tastes like heaven," Emily thinks to herself as she drinks from the two-liter bottle. Some days things just seem to work out right, and today is one of those days. After Jake fucked her good, she went to the manager's office to pay the room up for the week and for once the guy wasn't a fucking dick. Then she came back to the room and got fucked again. And Jake said they're gonna pull a couple thousand bucks for a quick trip down to Orange County. Yep, some days *things just go right*.

Emily finishes her long swig from the bottle and places it back on the floor next to her. She rolls toilet paper around her hand, wipes quickly, and flushes.

* * *

Reclining on the bed, Jake drops his cigarette butt into an empty beer can on the nightstand. The tobacco cherry sizzles out in the small remnant of beer inside. In the background, talk-show host Murray Levitch interrogates a female guest.

"So you're saying all he ever wants to do is smoke meth and have sex?" Murray asks incredulously.

Jake laughs sarcastically. "Yeah you dumb bitch that's what it's for!" he yells at the television.

The woman's face expresses a confusing mixture of sadness and excitement as she slowly nods at Murray.

"What the fuck is that look?" Jake angrily mimics the woman's nod. "Huh? What is that?"

"Well, I think you know what you need to do," Murray says sympathetically.

The sadly excited woman continues nodding.

"Let's bring him out!" Murray shouts.

The studio audience jeers as the man enters the stage and takes a seat next to the woman.

A remote flies through the air and hits the television. The channel abruptly changes to an *I Love Lucy* rerun. Lucy and Ethel are wrapping chocolates on an assembly line, trying desperately to keep up with an accelerating conveyor belt.

Jake's mood immediately improves. "Oh shit, they're tweekin!" he laughs.

As Lucy and Ethel stuff chocolates into their mouths, Jake examines his hands. He ignores the brown filth collected under his nails, instead focusing on the length of his right thumbnail—it's too long for his taste. Jake bites at the dirty nail as a toilet flushes.

Emily runs out of the bathroom with a big smile and jumps on top of Jake.

"Can you fuck me again baby?" she asks.

Still biting his thumbnail, Jake laughs and nods to the tv. "Look at Lucy tweekin," he says mid nibble.

Emily looks at the television and giggles, then rolls off Jake and trots over to the vanity. The vanity mirror keeps Lucy in view as Emily grabs a glass pipe and lighter from the cluttered counter. With her eyes fixed on Lucy's reflection, Emily raises the pipe to her lips.

"Ah-ah," Jake interrupts her, "nah, give it to me." He's still reclined on the bed, working his thumbnail.

Emily dutifully hands the pipe and lighter over to Jake, who stops biting his nail.

"Get dressed, we're driving to Orange County to make that cash I told you about." Jake presses the pipe against his lips.

Emily coos excitedly, "Ooh, what are we gonna do?"

Jake sparks the lighter and drags from the pipe. Wispy fingers of smoke rise from the bowl as Jake holds his breath.

"We're gonna steal a fucking dog," Jake says through an exhale.

Emily's eyes light up. "From where?"

"I'll show you."

Jake hands the pipe to Emily and grabs for his phone on the cluttered nightstand. He inadvertently knocks his beer can ashtray to the floor, near Emily's bare feet.

"Fuck!" Jake yells angrily as Emily drags from the pipe. He sits up and reaches for the can but Emily's in the way.

"Fucking get outta the way Emily!" Jake bumps Emily from her location and grabs the can. Ashy black beer soaks into the carpet.

"What the fuck," Emily angrily exhales, "Yeah you too you fucking dick!"

Jake crumples the can with a squeeze and stares wildly at her. "Don't start with me Emily, I'll fucking crush you," he threatens.

"Geez baby, I'm just joking," Emily says softly.

Jake backs off and puts the crumpled can back on the nightstand. He grabs his phone.

"This is where we're gonna get the fucker."

Jake shows Emily the Yelp page for Ruff Company Cut & Chew. She reviews it apprehensively.

"I don't wanna rob anyone Jake, come on," Emily whines.

"We're not robbing anyone Emily. We're just gonna go in, take a dog and leave. We're gonna snatch one of these fuckers getting a stupid haircut."

Emily laughs.

"Seriously Emily, these rich fucks take their dogs in to get perms and shit, getting their nails done. A dog!"

Emily laughs again as she warms to the idea.

"We're gonna take one of these pampered fucking mutts and just sell it right back to the stupid-ass owner, and then we're gonna do it again next week at another place."

"You think the owner will pay?" Emily trades Jake the pipe for the phone.

"Oh they'll pay, these rich fucks treat their dogs like kids!" Jake places the pipe to his lips and sparks the lighter. "Better than kids," he mutters, pipe pressed to his lips. Jake inhales deeply.

Emily scans the reviews for Ruff Company Cut & Chew:

> "Small shop with a very nice groomer."
>
> "They treat Chunky like the king that he is."
>
> "Great selection of treats and snacks. I'd give six stars if I could."
>
> "Terrible. My dog actually came back dirtier than I left him. Zero stars, never go there."
>
> "Best cobb salad in town!"

"Look at the pictures," Jake says haltingly, breath still held.

Emily scrolls through the pictures for Ruff Company Cut & Chew. A freshly groomed Maltese, hair tied up in a bow, smiles for the camera. Another image shows a happy poodle with the standard poofy-legged style.

Jake exhales, "You catch the one with the leg warmers?" He points at the poodle. "Jesus Christ these people," he remarks.
Emily laughs as Jake readies for another drag off the pipe.

"The place is real small so they can't have that many people there. All we gotta do is go in, grab a dog from the goddamn salon and leave."

Emily nervously pulls her stringy bangs down along her forehead. "Just go grab one?"

"Yep, just grab one. Grab one and leave Emily, that's all we gotta do." Jake sparks the lighter.

Emily continues pulling at her bangs as she studies the web page.

"Shouldn't we get one with a tag so we can call the owner for money?" she asks.

Jake, mid inhale, widens his eyes at Emily and nods emphatically. At the end of his toke, they swap pipe for phone again. Jake reexamines the pictures as Emily sparks the lighter.

"Fucking leg warmers," he says through held breath. "What's wrong with these people?"

Emily tries not to laugh as she too holds her breath.

Jake suddenly points at the television and exhales, "Oh fuck Emily, look! It's the dog people!"

An animal rescue commercial plays on the television. A scared terrier shakes in slow-motion as a caption solicits donations to an 800-number and web address.

Emily looks at the TV and immediately loses her breath in laughter.

"What the fuck is wrong with these people!" Jake says as he approaches the TV. He reaches out and touches the screen.

"Ohhh," Emily says sarcastically, "he wants his mommy!"

"Gimme a thousand bucks you little fucker," Jake taunts the on-screen dog, "then you can go back to your mommy!"

* *

Bobby's floppy ears fly upwards as he closes his eyes. Warm air flows past his snout, under his ears and down his chest.

"This is what it's like to be a bird," he thinks.

He's pretty sure Ms Lupe is speaking to him but he can't make out the words over the whir of the hair dryer. She moves the blower under him and Bobby lifts a leg to give her a better angle.

Before Dave, Bobby never got this treatment. His old owner made him sleep outside every night; in fact, he was never allowed in the house. Rain or shine, there he was out on the concrete. What most people don't understand is that the worst part of being outside is the goddamn fleas. Fleas were everywhere: on his snout, between his toes, around his wiener. He even had fleas deep inside his ears. Ever have a flea in your ear? Bobby had 'em, crawling around and biting all day and all night.

Now Bobby's with Dave, and Dave's the man. Every month or so, Dave'll break a flea pill up and mix it into Bobby's food. He thinks he's sly, but Bobby knows. Bobby knows a lot, in fact. He knows Dave needs a woman, and he knows that woman needs to be Ms Lupe. Every time Dave drops him off, Bobby sees the way they look at each other. And ol' Bobby can smell what's cookin' —dogs always can. Dave just needs to pull the trigger.

The dryer turns off. "Okay mijo, you all done."

An entry bell chimes from the front of the store.

Bobby's collar jingles as he shakes his ears out. He looks up expectantly at Ms Lupe.

"Aye, what you want little boy?"

Bobby edges over on the grooming table, placing his body next to Ms Lupe. He sticks his snout into her bosom. "Does that answer your question?" he thinks.

Lupe laughs and scratches Bobby under his chin.

A twitchy woman in a hoodie appears at the upper half of the grooming area's dutch door, ten feet from Lupe and Bobby. "Who's this tweeker bitch," Lupe wonders.

"You need something?"

Emily darts her eyes around the grooming area. She spots a few caged dogs in the far rear, a shampoo station off to the left, and Lupe and Bobby front and center at the grooming table

"I'm here to pick up my mom's pet dog," Emily says nervously. She flashes a gummy smile at Lupe.

"Oh yeah?" Lupe lowers her voice in challenge, "What his name is?"

Jake appears behind Emily and whispers in her ear. Lupe pulls Bobby closer.

"Shit's about to go down," Bobby thinks to himself. He lets a nervous bark fly towards Emily and Jake.

"Ha, that's him," Emily says. "You ready to go home boy?"

Bobby looks up nervously at Ms Lupe.

"You still not say what his name is." Lupe squares her shoulders to Emily and Jake. "You ain't taking this dog, you better get outta here or I gonna call the cops on you."

Mary, the feebly built owner of Ruff Company Cut & Chew, appears behind Jake and Emily. "Is there a problem here?" she asks timidly.

"They trying to kidnap a dog, Mary."

Jake suddenly grabs the door handle and opens it. "Get him!" he yells at Emily.

Emily rushes into the room as Jake stays behind and glares at Mary.

"That's my mother's dog," Jake tells Mary.

Mary's slow to process what's happening. She stares back at Jake, perplexed.

"You can't take–your mother has to come get the dog," Mary politely explains.

Emily approaches Lupe and Bobby. "Just give me the dog, I'm taking it to my mom!"

"Uh-uh, you not taking this dog from me puta!"

Bobby barks, "Get her Ms Lupe!"

"Give me the dog you beaner bitch!" Emily yells shakily.

Emily makes her move for Bobby. A heavy slap thuds into the side of her head. She staggers backward as Lupe comes forward. Another slap rattles her head.

"Kick her ass Ms Lupe!" Bobby barks.

Emily tucks her head as she retreats but Lupe grabs her hair.

"Help me Jake!"

"Yeah come on Jake, your ugly puta getting her ass kicked!"

Lupe's gone rogue. She jerks Emily sideways by the hair, clawing at her face. Emily flails her arms in a futile attempt to fight back.

Jake rushes into the room as Lupe continues her assault. He side-steps the two women and snatches Bobby by the scruff.

"Let's go!" Jake yells as he flees the grooming room with Bobby.

Lupe rips out a clump of Emily's hair. Freed from Lupe's grip, Emily quickly backpedals but Lupe latches on to her hoodie and starts feeding her uppercuts.

With the hoodie pulled over her head and Lupe's fist continually crashing into her face, Emily enters full desperation mode. She throws her arms forward and manages to reverse out of the hoodie as Lupe, still clutching the hoodie, falls backwards to the ground. Emily scrambles out of the room.

Outside, a run-down Toyota Camry sits parked with its rear facing the front entrance. Two crows circle overhead, using the car for target practice. A turd falls from the sky and lands smack dab in the center of the roof. Both birds caw excitedly.

Ruff Company's front door suddenly explodes open as Jake runs out with Bobby still held by the scruff. He opens the Camry's rear passenger door and hurls Bobby into the back before taking the driver's seat.

The store's front door flies open again as Emily runs to the car. She yanks the passenger door open and dives into the front seat as Jake nervously inserts the key in the ignition.

The front door bursts open once more. Lupe emerges, pissed off and wielding a huge beef bone.

"Hurry up Jake, she's crazy!"

Lupe rushes to the passenger side and swings her bone at the window. Emily covers her head.

THWACK!

The window remains intact but Lupe's raising the bone up for another swing.

"Hurry up Jake, go!"

Lupe's muffled voice calls through the window, "I gonna get you puta, you don't take my dog from me!"

Bobby barks at the window, "I'm back here, Ms Lupe!"

THWACK!

Lupe's bone strikes Emily's window again as the engine starts.

Jake shifts into drive and pulls away wildly. Bobby looks out the rear window and sees Ms Lupe shaking her bone at them.

"Don't worry mijo, Lupe gonna come for you!"

Bobby whines as Ms Lupe disappears from view. He looks at Jake and Emily in the front seats, both wild-eyed and drenched in sweat as they speed down the city street.

"Dave ain't going for this shit."

* * *

"Okay Ms Harris, I sprayed for those black widows and I also sprayed for crickets since they're a major food source for the spiders."

"Thank you Dave," Ms Harris replies with a warm smile.

"Here's the invoice." Dave hands her the pest control invoice. A chocolate Labrador suddenly appears at the door, barking excitedly at Dave.

"Coco, no!"

Ms Harris struggles to keep Coco inside but he squeezes past her and makes a friendly beeline for Dave. Dave kneels down with a smile and offers a fist for Coco to smell.

"Well hello, bud!"

"Sorry about that," a red-faced Ms Harris says.

Dave scratches Coco's chest, "Oh it's no problem at all, I love dogs. I have one of my own."

"Oh really?"

"Yep, a little mutt I adopted after I left the service."

"Ahh, what's his name?"

Dave smiles, "Bobby. My little boy."

Coco extends a paw and Dave shakes it.

"Well I'm sure Bobby's very sweet." Ms Harris loves it when people are friendly to Coco.

"Yep," Dave says. "Dogs have a nice way of keeping us crazy humans sane."

Ms Harris laughs, "That they do!"

Dave stands and gives Coco a final pat on the head. "Okay, well I'll see both of you next month then."

Ms Harris smiles. "We look forward to it! Come on Coco, let's get in the house now."

As Dave walks back to his utility truck, Coco walks into the house, happy at having made a new friend.

Dave enters his work truck and begins filing away Ms Harris' paperwork when his phone rings. The contact comes up on his phone as Dog Groomer; Bobby must be ready for pickup.

"Hello?"

"Hello," a shaky voice replies, "Is this Mr Sims?"

"Yes, this is him." Dave senses that this isn't the usual pickup call.

"Mr Sims, this is the owner of Ruff Company Cut & Chew. Um, there's been a situatio–"

"Is Bobby okay?" Dave instantly hits crisis mode.

"Well, not quite. Can you–"

"I'll be there in ten minutes."

Dave ends the call.

* * *

"Did they have any weapons?"

"No," Mary breathlessly tells Sgt Puckett.

Puckett makes a note in his report.

"Did they threaten you with anything?"

Mary shakes her head.

"So they just walked in and took the dog?"

Mary's too shaken up to answer. Lupe steps in.

"The bitch try to take the dog from me so I kick her ass."

Sgt Puckett smirks and makes a note.

"Then the guy come and grab the dog while she was getting her ass kicked."

Puckett continues jotting notes.

"So did they take anything else, or just the dog?"

"No, just the little doggy."

"Did they leave anything behind?"

"Yeah, that bitch left her hair behind cuz I ripped it out."

Puckett smirks again.

The door chime dings. Mary, Lupe and Puckett look up to see Dave enter. He walks directly to Sgt Puckett.

"Where's my dog?" Dave asks flatly.

"A hello would be nice," Sgt Puckett thinks to himself. He looks down at his notes and points a pen at Dave, "Mr Sims, right?"

"Yes."

"Mr Sims, someone stole your dog."

Dave quickly digests the information. "How do we get him back?"

"Well, um," Puckett searches for an answer, "we don't deal with things like this very often, Mr Sims."

"In fact," Puckett chuckles, "this is my first time encountering it."

Dave stares at Sgt Puckett.

"I'll be honest with you, Mr Sims, there's not much we can do. There's no weapon used, there's no actual robbery, and nothing was stolen besides the dog."

"Besides the dog," Dave repeats flatly.

Dave's smart attitude doesn't go unnoticed by Sgt Puckett. Jim Puckett's a sergeant for a reason, and when people disrespect his authority, he pushes back. Time for the big sarge to shut this one down.

"Yes Mr Sims, since it *is* just a dog, we're only looking at petty larceny. Let me ask, how much was the dog *worth*, Mr Sims?"

Dave glares at Puckett. Puckett returns the glare. An awkward second passes before Puckett breaks eye contact with a smirk.

"I'll file the report but I'll just be honest here and tell you that I can't imagine us devoting too much manpower looking for your dog, Mr Sims."

Puckett turns his attention to Mary. "Ma'am, can you sign this for me?"

Mary grabs Sgt Puckett's pen and signs the report.

"Thank you ma'am."

Puckett strolls to the front door.

"Mr Sims, I think your best bet is to put up flyers for your dog and try to get him back that way."

Puckett's suggestion is met with silence.

"Tough room," Puckett smugly remarks under his breath. He raps his knuckles twice on the door and exits the shop. The door chime dings.

Dave stands frozen in place as his head begins to spin. Lupe takes her shot.

"Sims, come here I gonna show you something." She beckons him to the groomer's room.

In a daze, Dave follows Lupe into the grooming area. Lupe picks up the hoodie Emily left behind and shows it to Dave.

"I didn't tell that pinche cop about it cause I gonna ask you first." She reaches into the pocket and pulls out a piece of paper folded multiple times.

Lupe hands the paper to Dave. He unfolds it.

> Jerry's Cloud Nine Motel
> Berdoo's Finest!
> Hourly–Daily–Weekly–Monthly rates

Dave quickly scans down to the bottom of the paper.

> Room 6
> $84 Weekly Rate
> Cash Payment – PAID IN FULL

Dave's face deadens as he glares at the receipt. His jaws clench into a vise.

Butterflies flutter in Lupe's stomach as she watches Dave's demeanor change.

"You gonna get 'em?" she asks quietly.

Dave turns his glare towards Lupe. He nods his head.

Lupe's eyes narrow at Dave. "I go with you," she tells him. "I gonna fuck that bitch up."

* * *

"Your hair is fucked," Jake laughs wildly through obnoxious smacks of chewing gum.

Emily's busy chomping her own stick of gum while inspecting her face in the visor mirror. Her nose is swollen and she has deep scratches along her cheeks and forehead. One scratch extends from her temple to her collarbone. The hair bangs she previously had look like they've been melted off with a curling iron.

She turns to Bobby in the back seat, "We better get a lot for you ya' little fuck."

Bobby, curled into himself, peeks out fearfully at Emily.

"Oh we will, we will," Jake smacks out the words. He turns around to Bobby, "That beaner bitch fought hard for you!"

Bobby's frightened eyes shift to Jake.

"Look how scared he is!" Jake says through wild laughter.

Jake shifts his attention back to the steering wheel. "And you better not fuck with me dog or I'll strangle you!"

Bobby sighs loudly, "You ain't gonna be so brave when Dave finds you."

Emily tears open a box of Twizzlers, "Come on Jake, you don't gotta be that mean to him."

"What? Look what he did to your face Emily!"

Emily bites off a piece of licorice. "He didn't do it, that stupid beaner did it."

"Same thing. She did it because of him, so fuck him and fuck her!" He eyes Bobby's curled body in the rear-view, "We better get paid for you fucker or I'm drowning you."

Emily slaps Jake's arm, "This is the exit, watch out!"

Car horns rage as Jake cuts across three lanes of freeway to make his exit.

A half mile into the desert, Jake pulls into the needlessly large parking lot of a 7-Eleven and parks far to the left of the store entrance, a good hundred feet away from the other vehicles. He turns off the engine and opens the car door.

Jake points at Bobby. "Don't let that fucker get away," he tells Emily.

Emily takes another bite of licorice as Jake steps out.

"Jake, what about food for the dog?"

"Give him licorice, we ain't gonna have him long."

Jake shuts the door and crosses in front of the car on his way to the store entrance. From the passenger seat, Emily watches Jake spit his gum to the ground and insert a fresh piece. She continues watching until her view is blocked by a black van pulling into the parking space alongside her.

* * *

Inside the 7-Eleven, Jake's eyes dart around as he stands behind a homeless guy using loose change to pay for a bottle of wine. His mind begins to race.

> cigarettes–cloves–menthols-reds
> candy bars–beef jerky–breath mints–chewing gum
> Clock says 6pm–6pm–6pm.
> I gotta get back to the room and get paid for this dog.
> energy pills-energy drinks–herbal supplements–condoms
> Fuck man, I'm tweeking bad.
> Gotta get back, gotta get back to the room and toke to calm down.
> lottery–scratchers–powerball–millions–licorice
> Why's this Habib-looking guy staring at me?

"Sir?" The thickly accented clerk prompts Jake for checkout.

Jake stares blankly at the clerk.

"What would you like to buy, sir?"

Jake snaps back to reality. "Burner phone and a pack of reds."

The clerk nods.

* * *

Exiting the store with his phone and cigarettes, Jake walks toward the location of the car but sees only a black van.

"Fuck, I'm tweeking bad," he thinks. "Where's the car and the dog?"

He cautiously approaches the ominous van. The large side window is tinted completely black. Jake's heart thumps in his chest as he reaches the van's side.

The van rocks slightly.

Jake's eyes widen to saucers. "Am I seeing shit or what?" he thinks.

He hears a muffled noise from inside the van. Again, the van appears to sway. Jake sneaks around to the rear and sees two windows, both blacked out.

"Mmmph!" comes a muffled noise.

"Dude, I think there's someone in there," Jake thinks. He stares into the rear windows, attempting to peer through the tint. The van rocks again.

"What the fuck," Jake says under his breath. His eyes bug as he desperately tries to see inside the van, but it's no use—the windows are solid black.

"*You wanna see inside?*" says a voice on Jake's right.

Startled, Jake drops his phone and cigarettes. He looks over and sees a white man in a pink collared shirt. Except for white tufts of hair on the sides of his head, the man is bald. He smirks deviously at Jake.

"You'll like it in there," the man says calmly. "It's very cozy."

Jake's heart pounds as he picks up his phone and cigarettes.

"N-n-no man, I'm just looking for my car."

The man continues smirking at Jake, who looks away from him and sees his car parked on the other side of the van—right where he left it.

The bald man laughs menacingly at Jake. "You can invite your friend. We'll play games."

Jake declines with a head shake and walks quickly to the car. He opens the door and jumps in.

"What took you so long?" Emily asks as she tries feeding licorice to Bobby.

"Emily stop fucking around, we gotta get outta here!" Jake says in a panic.

Emily responds with further panic, "What, why? Are the cops here?"

Jake quickly backs out of the parking space as the bald man scowls at him.

"No, we gotta get away from that weirdo!"

Emily sees the man scowling at Jake and flips him off. The man laughs wryly as Jake chirps his tires and hastily exits the parking lot.

* * *

Screams emanate from behind the door. High pitched, agonizing screams. Dave doesn't want to enter, but an unknown force compels him. He reaches for the doorknob and grabs it—the screams stop.

"Don't look," Dave tells himself. "You've done this before. Just go into the room and walk back out." He clenches his eyes and turns the knob. The door opens.

Dave takes a single timid step into the room; his foot squeaks against the slick floor. He cautiously shuffles further into the room, skating his feet against the floor to avoid slipping. His foot suddenly glides into something soft. Dave's blood runs cold. He blindly turns back to the entrance but realizes he's become disoriented inside the room.

"Open your eyes Dave," a voice in his head instructs. "Look at them."

Dave's pulse races. He shakes his head at the voice.

"Open your eyes, fucker," the voice warns. "Look what you've done to them."

Dave braces himself. He opens his eyes.

Charred mounds surround him. A child's doll lies twisted and burned in a corner. Below him, a gold bracelet glints on the blackened arm of an adult-sized mound. Nausea burns the inside of Dave's stomach as he fights the urge to vomit. He scans the room for an exit door but sees only walls.

"*Ma-an?*" a tiny voice calls out in Arabic.

Tears quickly well in Dave's eyes. "Please don't, I don't have any water."

"*Ma-an?*" the voice softly repeats.

The voice comes from the corner, near the doll.

"Don't make me go over there," Dave quietly pleads. "I don't want to go over there."

"*Ma-an?*"

Dave starts crying as the room shrinks. He's now next to the doll and can see that it's actually a young girl. The skin on her face is blackened and cracked, like a marshmallow held too long over a campfire.

"*Ma-an?*" the girl asks softly

"I told you," Dave pleads tearfully with the girl, "I don't have any water."

"Have I done something wrong, sir?"

Dave shuts his eyes and holds back a sob. He shakes his head.

"Why will you not look at me sir? Am I not pretty?"

Dave sobs.

"Why have you burned me sir? Have I done something wrong?"

"Stop!" Dave yells through tears.

A noise—movement—snaps his attention to the rear. A tall bearded man approaches with a machete. Dave, now armed with his Army-issued M4 carbine, takes aim and pulls the trigger. The firing pin clicks but the weapon jams. The tall man continues approaching, slowly and ominously. Dave clears the jam and squeezes the trigger. Again the rifle clicks, this time on an empty chamber. Dave looks into the bearded man's eyes—they burn with hatred for him.

The man swings his machete at Dave's head, narrowly missing. Dave lunges for his throat, grabbing it with both hands and pinning the man against the wall as the machete clinks to the ground. Punches hit Dave's arms as the man fights for life, but Dave's death grip is unbreakable. The man, rapidly weakening, tries for Dave's eyes but he easily defends it with a turn of the head. The bearded man, once tall, shrinks down as life leaves him. Dave lifts him by the throat and smashes his head into the floor.

A big-rig horn blares loudly. Other cars beep and honk as they angrily pass by. Rush-hour traffic has moved forward another hundred feet but Dave's stopped in the slow lane. His knuckles are white as he tensely grips the steering wheel. He looks at the in-car clock: 6pm. He looks over at Lupe. She smiles warmly at him.

"It's okay, Sims. We gonna get Bobby, then I gonna help you with everything."

Dave is embarrassed that Lupe saw him under one of his spells.

Lupe gently extends an arm towards the steering wheel and touches his hands. "Trust Lupe. I gonna help you get better no matter what."

FOR DOG AND COUNTRY

Dave nods silently at Lupe. He presses the gas pedal. They move forward together.

* * *

"*Ko-nee-chee-wa brothers and sisters!*"

Pipe in mouth, Jake laughs at the motel television. "This fucking guy is hilarious!"

A polished preacher with a strong tan smiles broadly at the camera. "Pastor Bart's on a healing tour of Japan right now, but why not stick around for some good ol' gospel music?"
Eyes fixed on the TV, Jake takes a drag from the pipe as Emily plugs the disposable phone into the wall to charge it.

"When are you gonna call for the money?" she asks.

Jake gestures with the pipe. "After this," he says with full lungs.

Bobby's turned tightly into himself near the front door, wishing he was on the other side of it. Jake glances over at him and exhales.

"Get the number off his collar," Jake instructs Emily.

Jake continues watching the TV preacher as Emily approaches Bobby and reaches down for his collar.

"Don't do it," Bobby growls, "you're not gonna like it."

Surprised, Emily pulls her hand back and laughs. She looks to Jake, whose attention has now fully shifted to Bobby. He nods at Emily to try again for the collar. Emily reaches down.

"I'll snap ya' one!" Bobby warns loudly.

Emily quickly pulls her hand back.

"Alright you little fucker," Jake says angrily as he steps to the bathroom vanity. He tosses the pipe on the counter and grabs a matchbook. "We gotta break him so he knows who the boss is," he tells Emily.

"Hey," Jake snaps his fingers at Bobby. "Hey dog, look at me."

Bobby peeks out from his tight coil.

Jake lights a match. Bobby's eyes widen. Jake throws it at him and Bobby springs to his feet.

"You like that?" Jake taunts.

He lights another match as Bobby cowers in the corner by the door. Jake crowds in on Bobby and throws it at him. Bobby flees to the vanity as Jake laughs.

Bobby remembers the matches from his nightmares. The kids from his past would torture him relentlessly with them. They'd press him down tight to the ground and light his tail on fire. They'd make him smell match smoke and laugh at him when he tried to turn away from it. He didn't have any friends back then, only mean dogs and meaner tormentors. Dave changed all that. Dave gave him pride, courage, and most importantly: Dave had his back. With Dave in his crew, Bobby had nothing to fear.

"Jake, come on, you don't have to tease him!"

"Shut up Emily, I'm teaching this fucker respect." Jake shifts over to Bobby's new cowering spot under the vanity and lights another match.

"Alright you nasty tweeker," Bobby growls loudly, "let's do this!"

Emily laughs at Bobby's growl. Jake throws the match at him—Bobby doesn't flinch.

"Oooh-hoo, we're gonna fight now, huh?" Jake says excitedly. He puts the matches back on the counter and crouches down to stare into Bobby's eyes. "Grrrr!" Jake growls.

Bobby growls back, "You ain't gonna like it when Dave comes busting through that door!"

Jake puts his hands out to Bobby's sides as Bobby watches alertly.

Jake feints his left hand at him—Bobby snaps and misses.

Jake feints again with the left—another snap hits air.

Jake feints left once more, then quickly darts in with his right hand and grabs Bobby's scruff. Bobby struggles to get his teeth on Jake's forearm but he can't reach it. Jake yanks Bobby out from under the counter.

"I got you motherfucker!" Jake says as he stands up with Bobby held by the scruff. He shows Emily, who applauds Jake's success. Bobby kicks his feet and squirms but Jake's grip is too tight.

"Oh look Emily," Jake says in mock disbelief, "this creature has a tail! Is it a beaver?"

Emily laughs giddily.

"Wait, no, I think it's a possum," Jake says sarcastically.

"It's a rat!" Emily says.

Jake raises his eyebrows at a giggling Emily.

"You're right Emily, it's a rat! A dirty, disgusting rat!"

With his free hand, Jake reaches around for Bobby's tail. He grips it tightly and releases the scruff.

Bobby's head swings toward the ground. Pain shoots into his rear as the weight of his body puts terrible pressure on his tail. Bobby cries out.

"Look what I caught Emily! A big ol' sewer rat!"

Emily laughs as Jake holds Bobby up by the tail. Jake swings Bobby left and right like a pendulum.

"Do you think he's learned yet?" Jake asks.

Upside-down, Bobby's head swings back and forth near Jake's jean-enclosed crotch. The skinny kid did this to him years ago. Bobby should have bit the kid in the balls back then but he was too afraid. Now the skinny kid's doing it to him again, but Bobby ain't afraid no more. Tonight, Bobby's tasting ballsack.

Bobby times the swing. Three. Two. One.

Chomp!

"Ahh!" Jake yells out. He immediately releases the tail but Bobby's latched on to his crotch.

"How's that for a sewer rat!" Bobby screams as he savagely shakes his head back and forth.

Jake falls to the ground with Bobby latched on. Bobby's gone feral, trying desperately to cut through the jeans and taste balls.

Emily can't believe her eyes. The previously timid dog is now a blur on Jake's crotch, and it's making noises she's never heard before. The dog sounds like something out of a horror movie

Jake reaches down and grabs at Bobby's neck. Bobby shakes him off as he keeps savagely twisting at his jeans. Inside is ballsack— inside is redemption.

Jake rolls to his side to get a better angle at the dog's neck. He reaches for it again and finally gets a grip on it with his right hand. He squeezes tight as Bobby continues going at his pants. Jake snakes his left hand around and manages a second, lighter grip on Bobby's neck. Bobby stops twisting but remains latched on to Jake's crotch. Ten seconds of inactivity pass. Jake gives Bobby a tug but the dog twists again. The two men are in a standoff.

"You want me to help?" Emily asks.

Jake shakes his head firmly. This is a delicate situation.

A full minute passes with Jake and Bobby both gripping each other tightly.

"I'm getting tired here Dave," Bobby thinks to himself. "I gotta let go. I can't do it."

Bobby releases.

With Bobby off of his crotch and clutched firmly by the neck, Jake immediately rolls to his knees and stands up. He raises Bobby's face to his own and stares darkly into the dog's eyes.

"Bye, fucker."

Bobby's eyes bulge as Dave tightens his grip. He can no longer breathe.

"Dave, where are you?" Bobby thinks. "I fought him Dave, just like you showed me. I fought him."

Bobby's eyes dim.

"I fought him Dave. I fought."

* * *

A dusty sun kisses the horizon as Dave and Lupe exit the freeway. They both peek at the phone navigator: six minutes remaining.

As they pass a 7-Eleven, Dave's phone rings from an unknown number. He wordlessly engages the speakerphone. Hushed, unintelligible voices are heard from the caller's end. A few seconds pass.

"I think they answered," a female voice whispers.

"Is this the owner of Bobby?" a man's voice asks. A dog collar jingles.

Dave glares at the phone.

"They didn't hear you," says the hushed female voice. "Ask again."

"Is this the owner of Bobby?" The collar jingles again.

Dave recklessly pulls to the side of the road and stops the truck.

"If you ever want to see—"

"Where's my dog?" Dave asks flatly.

Hushed excitement is heard from the caller's end.

"We have your dog. If you ev—"

"Where's my dog?" Dave repeats.

Quiet confusion is heard on the speakerphone.

"Listen to me. We have your—"

Dave ends the call. He and Lupe silently glare at the phone.

Dave abruptly exits the truck. Lupe looks in the driver-side mirror and sees him disappear behind the rear. He reappears in Lupe's mirror. She watches as he unlocks one of the compartments and reaches deep inside. He pulls out a large chrome pistol, closes the compartment and disappears back behind the truck. Lupe's face flushes as she awaits his return.

Dave gets back in the truck and lays the pistol on the bench between him and Lupe. He digs under his seat, removes a thick roll of duct tape, and tosses it next to the gun.

"Sims," Lupe says.

Dave, dead-eyed, looks at her.

Brow lowered, she slowly drags a finger across her throat.

Dave looks back at the road. He shifts into gear and floors the gas as Lupe grabs the duct tape.

* * *

Jake and Emily stare down at the bed. The message on the phone is loud and clear: *Call Ended.* Neither of them wants to speak first. Emily starts crying.

"Why'd you have to kill the dog!?" she yells as she walks to the vanity.

"What does it matter Emily!?" Jake rotates the collar in his hand.

"Because we can't sell a collar, Jake!" Emily picks at her face in the mirror as tears flow.

"Just hold on, we gotta think!" Jake moves next to Emily and draws a line of meth out on the counter.

"That guy's gonna kill us Jake!"

"He's not gonna kill us Emily," Jake says nervously, "we used a burner phone! He doesn't know who the fuck we are."

"He's gonna kill us Jake," she sobs, "you killed his dog and now he's gonna kill us."

Jake snorts the line. "Would you shut the fuck up! We have to think!"

Emily whimpers, "I lost my jacket, Jake."

"What? What are you talking about?" Jake asks shakily.

"The beaner took my jacket," she cries. "I couldn't remember where I put it," Emily chokes, "but now I remember." She dry heaves into the sink.

"Stop being paranoid, they can't trace a jacket!"

A vehicle screeches to a stop just outside the door. Jake's eyes widen in fear.

"He's gonna kill us Jake!" Emily screams.

Vehicle doors slam closed. Jake runs to the front door and peeks through the eyepiece. A man in a beige uniform is back-lit against the setting sun, accompanied by the lady from the groomer. The man in the uniform approaches the door with a gun in his hand.

Jake motions to Emily in a panic, "Help me hold the door!"

Emily screams, "We're gonna die!"

Jake shoulders up against the door and looks through the eyepiece again. The man rears back and kicks the door with a heavy thud.

"Emily help!"

Another thudding kick hits the door. Wood crunches as the jamb splinters at the doorknob. Emily screams.

The kicking stops. Jake quietly peeks out and sees the man raising his pistol to the eyepiece. Jake quickly drops down into the corner.

BAM! The eyepiece explodes into the room.

CRACK! The door flies open and slams into Jake's head. In walk Dave and Lupe.

"Hey puta," Lupe points at Emily, "I look familiar huh? Remember when you call me the bad word?" Lupe pulls out a long, noisy leader from the duct tape. "I gonna fix you today bitch!"

Emily curls into a ball on the ground as Lupe makes a beeline for her. Dave looks to his right and sees Jake bleeding from the forehead in the corner, hands opened in peace towards Dave.

Dave points the gun at him, "Where's my dog?"

Jake can't think of a response. Dave kicks him in the face.

"Put your arms together puta," Lupe demonstrates by placing her own forearms side-by-side, elbows and wrists touching.

Emily, broken and sobbing, complies. Lupe loops the tape roll around her arms, working from elbow to wrist.

"Where's my dog?" Dave asks again.

Jake brings his hands together defensively, "I got your dog man!"

Dave kicks him in the face again.

"Okay, you good," Lupe says as she finishes wrapping Emily's arms together. She tears off a new strip of tape. "Now I gonna wax that mustache for you," Lupe says. She presses the strip tightly across Emily's upper lip.

Dave grabs Jake by the collar and drags him toward the vanity.

"Come on man, I got your dog!" Jake pleads.

"Okay puta, this gonna sting a little." Lupe rips the tape off Emily's lip.

Emily yelps in pain. Blood flows from her red, raw skin.

"That's better, you don't look like a man no more."

Dave drags Jake over and seats him next to Emily.

"Okay cabron, put your arms together," Lupe instructs.

Jake reluctantly puts his hands together.

Lupe raises her voice, "No, jor *arms*!"

Jake looks confusedly at Lupe. She quickly demonstrates and Jake copies her.

"*Pinche baboso*!" Lupe laughs derisively at Jake, glancing at Dave and shaking her head. She begins taping Jake's arms together.

"Where's my dog?" Dave asks flatly.

"I left him with my friend man," Jake pleads. "I'll call my friend and he'll bring your dog."

"Put your legs straight cabron," Lupe tells him.

Jake straightens his legs out in front of him. Lupe quickly tapes them together.

Jake watches Dave walk to the room phone and disconnect it from the wall.

"Okay you done cabron. Don't go nowhere," Lupe giggles to herself. She turns her attention back to Emily. "Okay, I do your eyebrows now—that one you got look ugly." Lupe rips off a piece of tape.

Dave grabs the phone and walks over to Jake. He rears back and hurls the phone at Jake's face. Jake's nose explodes in a bloody mist.

Lupe tears tape away from Emily's eyebrows. Emily whimpers.

"Oops, they both come out. Now you got none like my cousin —she a puta too."

"Where's my dog?" Dave repeats his monotone question.

Blood streams from Jake's nose and forehead. He begins to cry and shake his head in defeat as he sits immobilized on the floor, his arms and legs bound tightly with tape. "I'll get him man, just give me a chance."

Dave turns and walks out to his truck. The tenants from next door are huddled together outside, wondering what the commotion is. Dave raises a finger to his lips and the tenants return to their room. He opens a compartment on the side of his truck.

At the vanity, Emily's eyes are closed as she cries to herself. Lupe smacks her in the head, "Hey puta, open your eyes I gotta show you something."

Emily opens her tearful eyes. "Please don't," she pleads with Lupe.

"Puta look at me, you gotta see this."

Lupe points at Emily's t-shirt. "Those"—Lupe raises her eyebrows—"are the worst titties I ever seen."

Emily closes her eyes and continues crying.

"I think I can fix 'em." Lupe looks at Jake, "What you think, cabron? I gonna put tape on 'em and pull 'em out." Lupe makes a pulling motion with her arms.

Jake stares in dismay as Lupe studies Emily's chest.

"*Aye aye aye,*" Lupe shakes her head in disgust, "how you can fuck that thing, cabron?"

Dave enters the room lugging a large red can and a metal bug sprayer. He drops them to the floor with a thud. Stenciled on the side of the bug sprayer are the words *Eleven-Bravo Pest Exterminators.*

"Uh-oh, you both in trouble now," Lupe warns.

Desperation floods Jake's eyes. "I can call man, just let me call!"

Dave yanks the bedspread off the bed and drags it to the vanity. Lupe helps him wrap it around Jake and Emily's bodies. Dave grabs a towel from the counter and wraps it snug around Jake's neck. Lupe follows suit, wrapping a towel around Emily's neck. Dave then flips a switch on the wall—the bathroom's exhaust fan whirs into action.

"Five minutes tops!" Jake pleads. "I'll have your dog here in five minutes!"

Dave unscrews the top of the bug sprayer, then unscrews the top of the large red can. He pours the contents of the red can into the bug sprayer. Gasoline vapors fill the air. Dave replaces the can tops, then grabs the bug sprayer and approaches Jake.

"Where's my dog?"

Dave sprays Jake's face with gasoline as Jake attempts a gurgled response. He pumps the sprayer and coats Jake's entire head, then soaks the towel around his neck.

Lupe looks at Emily, "Where Bobby at, huh puta?"

Dave turns to Emily and sprays her face up and down. She chokes and heaves. He walks back to the front door and places the sprayer down, then casually walks back to the vanity and grabs the matchbook off the counter.

Sirens approach in the distance. Lupe posts herself at the front door as a lookout.

Dave looms over Jake and presents a choice to him. In one hand, Dave displays the pistol. In the other, the matchbook. Jake reviews his options—bad or worse.

"Where's my dog?"

Jake shakes his head in hysterics.

Dave steps backwards and lights a match. Terror invades Jake's eyes. Dave tosses the match at Jake's feet—it burns out.

Dave pulls another match from the book. Jake, jaw clenched, grunts in fear.

"WHERE'S MY DOG!" Dave yells at him.

Jake makes his choice. "He's in the dumpster!" Jake sobs. "I threw him out in the fucking dumpster man!"

Lupe looks into the room. Dave takes one further step backwards. He strikes the match as Jake's eyes flash in the background. Dave touches the match to the others—they loudly ignite into a single flame. He tosses the flaming matchbook at Jake's head.

"Wait man no—"

Flames whoosh to life around Jake's head. Emily's head whooshes next. In unison, they scream.

Dave and Lupe watch as the comforter catches fire, fully engulfing Jake and Emily in flames. Their dying screams mix with the sound of approaching sirens. Dave backs away from the inferno to stand next to Lupe in the doorway.

Dave turns to Lupe. She turns to him.

"Thank you Lupe," Dave says. He puts the pistol to his head and pulls the trigger.

* * *

Butterflies fly wild in a green field. Giant yellow sunflowers gently sway as a rainbow paints the sky. Hummingbirds and honeybees buzz from one flower to the next. At the field's center, Bobby runs.

He runs, and runs, and runs.

Murder, American Style

San Antonio is where the voice told him to go. He obeyed it and now he's here, inside *Phil's Flags and Firearms*, looking for a shirt with an American flag on it. The only one he can find features a half-American / half-Texan flag collage.

"Look at the back," the voice tells him.

Eighteen-year-old Johnny Jyde turns the shirt around. The words *Don't Mess With Texas* are embraced by a huge set of cattle horns.

The voice giggles inside his head. Johnny giggles too.

"Now get a pair of cowboy boots and a big ol' fuckin' hat," the voice tells him.

Johnny grins as he strolls the wall of boots. He spots a pair with a garish American flag design.

"Perfect, Johnboy. You'll fit in real nice with them good ol' boys."

Johnny nods to himself. He finds his size on the rack and slips them on. Perfect fit. He leaves his sneakers under the bench— he won't need them anymore.

"Hurry up Johnny, we got work to do boy."

Johnny quickly finds a stars-and-stripes cowboy hat and mashes it onto his head. He steps in front of a full-length mirror and eyes himself up and down.

"You look like a fucking idiot," the voice in his head chuckles. Johnny chuckles too.

On second glance, Johnny notices that something about his outfit seems off. It clicks—he needs a belt buckle.

"Smart boy, Johnny. Hurry up you fucking nutjob."

Johnny grabs the biggest, gaudiest hunk of metal he can find on the belt rack, a buckle stamped with the words *2ⁿᵈ Amendment– The Right to Bear Arms.*

"Alright, put your serious face on and go get a nice toy. Now is not the time to crack."

Johnny heads to the gun counter. The clerk behind the counter wears an outfit nearly identical to his own.

The curious clerk points at Johnny's clothing, "You fixin' to pay for all that here?"

Johnny nods; his flag-covered hat nods with him.

"'Kay then, just gimme a sec to look at 'ya."

The clerk inspects Johnny's outfit.

"'Merican flag hat," he drawls as he punches the price into the register. The register chings.

"'Merican flag boots."

Ching.

"Tex'merican shirt."

Ching.

"Gun buckle."

Ching.

"That gonna be all, son?" the clerk asks.

Johnny points at a rifle on the wall, "I'll take the AR-15 too."

* * *

Johnny exits Phil's Flags and Firearms with the AR-15 slung over his shoulder, barrel pointing towards the ground. Before him stands a large, orderly formation of white men, all armed, all angry and all facing a stage where a barely attractive blonde woman barks through a megaphone. She's flanked on one side by six white cowboys. On her other side, a single black cowboy stands tall.

"Cause it's a *fact* that guns are the foundation of this great country!" the blonde lady's amplified voice yells.

The horde of men cheer as one. The formation's rear is filled with clean cut men wearing wraparound sunglasses, each shoulder slung with an assault rifle.

The voice in Johnny's head speaks, "There's an open place for you in the middle of 'em all, Johnboy. Go stand there."

Johnny discreetly makes his way into the outside ranks of the horde. In his head-to-toe flag camouflage, he goes unnoticed.

"Now maybe the *liberals* wanna tell y'all somethin' different," the blonde lady shouts sarcastically.

The horde rumbles with boos.

Johnny's arrived at the meaty layer of the horde. Surrounding him are chubby middle and senior-aged men wearing caps on top of liver-spotted heads. Pistols are stuffed into holsters strapped tightly to their fat hips.

"But the fact is, them *liberals're* wrong!"

Johnny cuts through the cheering flesh of the horde to an open spot in the middle of the formation. He stands next to a man whose soft, pear-shaped body looks like a water balloon. He wears very thick, very square transition glasses whose lenses have turned dark gray in the sunlight. A massive Desert Eagle sits in a holster on his shapeless hips.

"Look at 'em all," the voice tells Johnny. "Aren't they the fucking grossest things you've ever seen?"

Johnny giggles as he inspects the central horde surrounding him. Wet armpits, leathery skin, walrus mustaches and fat bodies dominate. Hip holsters, shoulder holsters, and even a few ankle holsters contain handguns of every shape and size. The stench of body odor and flatulence is nearly overwhelming where he stands.

"And if they don't like my guns," the blonde lady barks, "they can come and git it!"

The horde erupts in sarcastic laughter. Johnny hears multiple *yee-haws* shouted behind him.

The lady mimics a wrestling taunt, slamming knife-edged hands on her crotch as she thrusts her hips forward.

"That transplant bitch is a fake, Johnny," the voice tells him. "Her accent is fake but they're eatin' her right up."

Johnny observes the dolled-up lady strutting around the stage in western wear and caked-on makeup. She slams her crotch again and thrusts her hips. A bloated man in front of Johnny tilts his head back and emits an ear-piercing rebel yell into the breeze. Others follow suit. The horde sounds like a pack of horny hyenas crying in the night.

"I got just one question for all y'all," she shouts through the megaphone.

The man with the water-balloon body leans over to Johnny and nods toward the black cowboy onstage. "I don't trust the colored one," he whispers.

The singular black cowboy gives his six-shooter a practice twirl before shoving it back into his hip holster.

Through the gray tint of his square lenses, the water-balloon man winks at Johnny.

"Who here likes *open carry*?" the blonde lady asks the horde.

Laughter and excited shouts call back to her.

"Johnny, listen to me!" the voice in his head commands.

Johnny concentrates on the voice.

"They have to die, Johnny."

"And who here loves 'Merica!?" she yells to the crowd.

More excited shouts call back.

"All of them, Johnny."

"On the count of three," the blonde lady yells, "I want all y'all to raise them beautiful, God-given guns up in the air!"

"They're a virus that has to be wiped out, Johnny."

"One!" she yells.

"Do exactly as I say and we'll finish 'em off."

"Two!"

Chubby, sweaty hands clench gun handles, ready to draw.

"Three!"

Metal slides against plastic and leather as the horde raise their guns in unison.

The voice yells at Johnny, "Point at the stage and yell the word shooter—do it now!"

"Shooter!" Johnny gestures toward the stage.

The horde instantly goes on full alert, scanning for the gunman called out by Johnny. The water-balloon man next to him already has a target in mind. He looks down the sight of his Desert Eagle and takes aim at the black cowboy.

BOOM!

The black cowboy's head explodes in a splash of red.

"Shooter!" a man's voice yells from the stage. The remaining cowboys aim their six-shooters at the water-balloon man. Synchronized cowboy-shootin' action sends thirty-six bullets into his soft, pear-shaped body. The man crumbles to the ground. To Johnny's surprise, water leaks out from the holes in his body.

"We openly carry our guns 'cause it's our *got-dang* 'Merican right to do so!" the blonde lady yells, oblivious to the bedlam unfolding all around her.

"Shooter!" a voice yells from the rear of the horde.

Rifle fire whizzes past Johnny's head on its way to the stage. The cowboys plink down one-by-one like targets in a shooting gallery.

Johnny looks down at the crumpled man next to him and laughs as his body leaks water—he was a water balloon all along!

"Take my gun, boy," the man gasps. His body is quickly deflating.

"We carry our guns," the blonde lady yells, "to protect against the *queers*!"

"Shooter!" a pair of voices sing on Johnny's left.

The source of the voices, two fat-bodies being strangled by their jeans, execute a slow, unathletic combat roll that ends with a thud as they fail halfway through. The men grab their backs in pain.

Bullets crack and whiz past Johnny in every direction. He stands at the center of the quickly shrinking horde, looking down at the water-balloon man as he rapidly deflates.

"Give my gun," the man gurgles, "to my son."

"We carry our guns to protect against the *Jews*!" the blonde lady continues. Shouts and gunfire are sporadic now.

"Tell him to kee—*aurglegurgle*," the balloon man chokes and spits water from his mouth. From deep behind his thick gray lenses, the man's desperate eyes plead with Johnny. He's mustering his energy for one final push—one final message for Johnny to deliver to his son.

"We carry our guns," the blonde lady yells, "to protect against the *chinks*!"

"Tell my son," the man strains, "to keep it in the family-*y-y*." His lips flap and fart on his life's final word. All water has left him; His once pear-shaped body is now flat.

"And most of all—"

The blonde lady pauses. She and Johnny are the only people left standing.

"Most of all, we carry our guns to protect against the *niggers*!"

"She's vile, Johnny!" the voice says. "Kill her!"

Johnny raises his AR-15 and aims for center mass. He squeezes off a round.

"Wake up Johnny," the blonde lady yells at him, "take your pill!"

Johnny fires another round at her.

"Johnny, wake up and take your pill!" she says.

"Kill her Johnny!" the voice says.

He unloads the whole magazine at her with no effect.

"Get up and take your damn pill Johnny!"

* * *

"Get up and take your damn pill Johnny!"

Johnny opens his eyes and sits up in bed.

"Take your pill, Johnny!" his mom yells from the bedroom doorway.

"Yeah okay," Johnny says as he rubs the sleep from his eyes.

Johnny's mom sneers at him before disappearing down the hall.

"*Today's the day, Johnboy,*" the voice in his head says.

Johnny hears a new voice in his head. "No, today's not the day, John. Just take your pill and go to school."

"The pill makes you dead inside, Johnboy. Throw it out."

"No John, that's not true," the new voice argues. "You need your pill to be normal John, you know that."

Johnny grabs his pill from the nightstand and stares at it.

"Normal you is *without* the pill, Johnny. That bitch mom is the one who put you on it. She's the one who brought you all the way out here to Texas. Today's the day, Johnboy!"

"John, you know you'll feel better after you take your pill. Take it now, then you can ask someone at school for help getting your head straight."

"The school's the problem!" the voice yells. "They'll throw you in jail, Johnny! Throw that fucking pill away and let's follow the plan!"

"Today is not the day, John. Just take—"

Johnny throws the pill into a cluttered corner of his bedroom. It disappears from sight.

"*Good boy, Johnny.*"

Johnny takes a deep breath.

"Get your backpack out of the closet," the voice instructs.

Johnny opens his closet door. Hidden underneath a jacket is an unzipped backpack filled with loaded rifle clips. He grabs one before zipping the bag closed and heaving it onto his bed.

"Get your toy, Johnboy."

Johnny reaches towards the rear of the closet and grabs his AR-15.

"Remember when your grandpa gave you this fucking thing for your birthday?"

Johnny scowls at the rifle.

"Remember when he forced you to shoot it, even after you told him you hate guns?"

Johnny walks to his bed and sits down with the rifle.

"Remember when that racist bitch told you she was taking you to Texas so she could keep you away from all the niggers and queers in California?"

Johnny nods to himself.

"Today you erase them, Johnny."

Johnny discreetly inserts the magazine into the rifle. It clicks softly.

"You're gonna be famous today, boy."

Johnny hears his mom walking down the hallway. She passes his room without looking in.

"Kill her Johnny. Kill your grandpa next. Then kill everyone in the school."

Johnny giggles quietly to himself.

"Kill 'em all, Johnny."

Johnny quietly pulls the charging handle back on the rifle and releases it.

"You're going in the history books today, Johnboy."

Johnny smiles to himself.

"Hey mom, come here I wanna show you something!"

Joey

Joey caught a good one today and boy, does he need it. The last few weeks have been filled with chatty homebodies requesting all manner of electrical work, from replacing breaker panels to installing GFCIs to setting up nanny cams. On top of that, he spent a couple nights on a band gig for that lying-sack-of-shit TV preacher. This week offered him a break and he spent the first day of it engaging in his favorite hobby: fishing.

It didn't take long to hook one—she practically jumped right into the boat. He considered trying for another but decided to quit while he was ahead. The world's full of fish, no need to get greedy.

As Joey pulls off the freeway, excitement flutters in his stomach. He hasn't caught a fish in over a month; Meanwhile, life's little stresses have steadily accumulated into a boulder resting heavily on his shoulders. Today's success has already lightened that load and, before the night is through, Joey will be able to breathe again.

A half mile down a desert road, Joey pulls his van into the gravelly parking lot of a 7-Eleven. This particular shop, way out here in the desert, is Joey's go-to spot after a good day fishing. Except for the store clerk and the crows hanging out on the roof, nobody knows he comes here. He's friendly with the clerk, and as for the crows: Who gives a fuck?

Joey cruises over to his regular spot tucked away in a corner of the lot and finds a car parked there. He watches as a tweeker leaves the car and walks toward the storefront. Joey pulls alongside the car and puts the van in park. He peeks over at the car on his left —inside is a chick tweeker and her dog.

Joey steps through the black curtains separating the seats from the rest of the cabin. The van's rear is spacious, carpeted, and very dark due to the blackout curtains covering the passenger-side and rear windows, themselves tinted black. Knives of every shape and size hang ominously from the carpeted walls. A well-worn office chair is positioned at the side window, its seat swiveled inward toward the driver's side of the van. Directly across from the chair, a shackled woman lies naked and motionless on the floor. Her wrists are cuffed together and secured tightly to a loop of chain around her waist. Another chain runs from her waist down to the cuffs around her ankles; the chain's short length locks her legs into a slight bend. A padlock secures the waist chain to an eyebolt rising through the carpet next to the woman's hip. The woman is immobilized and, with a ball-gag in her mouth, muted.

Joey crouches next to his captive and glares into her terrified eyes. "I'm coming back in thirty seconds. *You shut your fucking mouth.*"

The frightened woman nods her head.

Joey lingers over her, unblinking. She nods again.

Satisfied that he's made his point, Joey passes through the curtains to enter the front cabin. The van door clunks closed as Joey heads for the store.

* * *

Joey stands behind the tweeker, watching him fidget around in the purchase line as a wino at the counter pays for his purchase with dimes and quarters. The back of the tweeker's shaved head is full of scabs. "What a miserable bastard," Joey thinks. "I should put him out of his misery."

The homeless man at the counter finishes his purchase and heads for the door. It's the tweeker's turn to pay but he's still fidgeting around like a nervous bird. Joey glares at the back of his head.

"Sir?" the clerk prompts the tweeker.

The tweeker snaps to attention and steps up to the counter. He mumbles something to the clerk; the clerk acknowledges and deftly grabs a disposable phone and pack of cigarettes from the shelf behind him. The tweeker pays for his items and hurries to the door.

"Joe, my friend!" the thickly accented clerk says with a broad smile.

Joey grins, "Staying cool in here, Mo?"

"Oh Joey man," discomfort paints Mo's face, "it's been so hot this week, very hot!" Mo casually grabs a pack of Menthol cigarettes from the shelf and places them on the counter. He knows what Joey likes.

Joey reaches for his wallet, "You should cool down with a Slurpee, Mo."

Mo reaches under the counter and pulls out a half-empty Slurpee cup. "Way ahead of you brother," Mo chuckles. He wraps his lips around the straw and sucks—the straw darkens as it fills with Slurpee.

Joey laughs and puts a twenty-dollar bill on the counter.

Mo quickly chokes down his mouthful of crushed ice, wincing as the cold freezes his mouth. "How was the fishing today, Joe?" Mo's voice barely makes it out of his frozen throat.

Joey laughs again, "I caught a good one today, Mo."

Mo's eyebrows raise in delight. "You see Joe! Last time you come in I tell you," Mo's voice softens, "just be patient."

Joey nods and grabs his cigarettes from the counter.

"And now," Mo raises his shoulders, "you catch a good one."

Joey points at him, "What can I say? You're good luck, Mo."

Mo cocks his head. "Maybe, maybe," he says softly.

A leathery old man lines up behind Joey.

"Keep the change Mo—I'll be back in later for a Slurpee."

A laugh flies out of Mo as Joey heads for the exit. The old man steps forward as Mo watches Joey leave.

"Oh man," Mo laughs heartily as he greets the new customer. "My friend Joe," Mo nods at the front door, "such a sweet guy."

* * *

Liza's eyes have adjusted to the darkness inside the van. Black curtains shield the side and rear windows, with only the faintest shadow of light falling on the floor below them. A long black case lies on the floor near the rear doors. The whole interior, including the walls and ceiling, is covered in black carpet. Sinister knives hang from the walls—she avoids looking too closely at them.

Liza knows she's in deep shit with this guy but she's trying her best to stay calm and think clearly to figure a way out of this mess. It's only been a few hours since the bald guy picked her up, she's still alive and he hasn't raped her. If she's lucky, maybe the most he'll do is fuck her and let her go. Just please don't use a knife on her. Don't cut her. *Please don't.*

Liza closes her eyes and prays, "Please God, let me get out of this. I'll stop hooking and get a real job and do anything you want, just don't let me die. I'm okay if he rapes me, just don't let him kill me. Please don't let him cut me. Amen."

Liza opens her eyes and finds them focused on the blade of a long, jagged knife hanging on the wall beside her. She imagines the cold blade being used in the worst ways in the worst places. She imagines it poking and ripping into her body, tearing her skin apart as her own blood gushes out. Anchored to the floor and gagged, she feels like she can't breathe. A wave of cold suddenly washes over her. As panic sets in, Liza begins to thrash and scream.

* * *

The 7-Eleven door closes behind Joey as he heads toward his van. In the distance, he spots the tweeker looking in the van's rear windows. Joey quickly surveys the parking lot: a few people come and go but nobody pays any attention to his van or the tweeker. Joey quietly approaches him and notices the van rocking slightly. The tweeker continues peering through the windows as Joey creeps to within a couple feet of him.

"*You wanna see inside*?" Joey asks.

The tweeker nearly jumps out of his skin as he drops the items in his hand.

"You'll like it in there," Joey smirks ominously at the tweeker. "It's very cozy."

* * *

Liza freezes. From somewhere near the van's rear, she hears the muted voice of the bald guy. She listens closely—again his voice carries into the van, but it's faint and unintelligible. She hears him laugh. It sounds like he's talking to someone.

Liza considers screaming out but she knows the ball-gag almost completely muffles her and she's not even sure if another person is out there. The last thing she wants to do is anger the bald guy. She has to be smart about this.

"If I hear a clear voice anywhere near me," she tells herself, "I'll take my chance and scream."

Her eyes light up as a car door closes near her side of the van. Someone else is definitely over there—maybe even the police.

Heart thumping in her chest, Liza takes a deep breath and readies herself. Once she hears a clear voice, she's screaming bloody murder.

The dampened sound of a chugging car engine fills Liza's ears. She follows the sound of the car as it moves rearward, then squeals away into the distance. A much louder sound replaces it—the sound of the van's driver-side door creaking open.

"No!" she thinks. "This isn't happening!"

The door thunks closed. Liza closes her eyes to shut out the world. The van engine turns over; cool air blows into the cabin. She hears someone pass through the front curtain. A presence looms over her. Liza keeps her eyes shut.

"Please God," she cries inside, "make this go away."

Liza hears a mechanical click far above her, near the ceiling. Someone sits down in the office chair across from her—air whooshes from the seat cushion. Cellophane crinkles as an item is unwrapped. A Zippo lighter clicks open, then snaps closed. Cigarette smoke fills the cabin.

"Open your eyes," growls a voice from the chair.

The voice startles Liza. She'd hoped this would all go away—it didn't. She opens her eyes to a cabin bathed in red from an overhead light. The bald guy sits in the chair, smoking a cigarette and glaring at her. Liza softens her eyes at him in an attempt to gain his sympathy.

As red light casts down on the man, Liza gets her first chance to see just how creepy he really is. Broad tufts of white hair grow along both sides of his head, but the rest of his scalp is completely bald. His face wears a permanent scowl. His eyes, black and unflinching, stare through her. She never would have got in a van with a guy this weird—not in a million years—but he was wearing a ball cap when he picked her up and looked like a normal guy.

"You're gonna die tonight," the man says gruffly.

Liza swallows hard.

"I'm gonna strangle the life out of you. I'm gonna watch you struggle, and I'm gonna enjoy every second of it.

Tears flow from Liza's eyes. The bald guy's cigarette glows red as he takes a drag.

"And when you're down to your last breath, I'm gonna suck it right outta your lungs. Your last breath belongs to me."

Liza closes her eyes and cries.

"Open your eyes."

Liza defiantly shakes her head and sobs.

"Open your eyes," he warns, "or I'll cut 'em out."

Liza looks at the bald guy as tears pour from her eyes. She momentarily chokes on the ball-gag.

"You need to pay attention from here on out. This is your last hour of life." The man points a stern finger at her, "Keep your eyes open. Do you understand me?"

Liza nods sadly.

The man takes a final drag from his cigarette before extinguishing it in a flip-down ashtray next to the window. He leaves his chair and crouches down next to Liza as she tenses in fear.

Liza looks up at him; his dark eyes stare into hers. Bound, gagged and secured to the floor, she's utterly helpless beneath him. Her chest heaves in fear as the man's unflinching eyes pierce her own.

"Please stop," her eyes beg him, "I don't like it."

The bald guy pounces on Liza's fear, unleashing further evil through his glare. Liza squirms beneath him as her pulse races out of control. He shoves a hand into his pocket—Liza's heart skips a beat. The man pulls out a key and opens the padlock locking her waist to the floor.

"Sit up," he commands.

Hands still shackled and bound to her waist, Liza awkwardly orients herself into a seated position, fearful of what comes next.

"Pick something from the wall," the man gestures at his collection of knives.

Liza emphatically shakes her head as fresh tears flow. The bald guy suddenly grabs her hair and yanks her head backwards.

"Listen to me," he glares at her, "either you're gonna pick one or I'm gonna pick one."

Vision blurred by tears, Liza searches the red-tinted wall. From long blades with hooked ends to short blades with jagged edges, every knife looks bad when she imagines it cutting her. She tries to find a short, straight one without any nasty edges. She spots a dagger and nods to it. The bald guy removes it from the wall and holds it close to her face to inspect. Liza winces.

"I'm gonna remove your gag. If you scream or yell, I'll cut your head off with this knife."

He yanks her head back again, forcing her to look up at him. "Even if you scream, you will not be saved. I will cut your head off before anyone makes it inside this van."

Eyes latched to hers, he pauses to let the message sink in. "Do you understand?"

"His eyes are so mean," Liza thinks despairingly. She nods at him.

The bald guy tosses the knife to the floor next to his chair, on the side furthest from Liza. He loosens the strap on her gag, pulling the ball from her mouth and placing it underneath her chin. Liza is immediately relieved with the ball removed; she can finally close her jaw and swallow normally.

The man sits down in his chair, facing Liza. "Come over here next to me," he says while patting his left leg.

Liza scoots over to the man's side, conscious of the knife resting on the other side of him. She considers grabbing the knife and attacking him, but her hands are still bound tightly to her waist. There's no way she can grab it without him knowing and even if she had it in her hands there's nothing she could do with it. She needs to free her hands before she can use the knife.

The bald guy slides the curtain open on the black-tinted side window. Liza sees that they're in a 7-Eleven parking lot and they're parked far away from the store entrance. Beyond the parking lot, a vast, lonely desert stretches out to the horizon. Liza watches a stranger enter the store, oblivious to the van and the events occurring inside it.

"Do you remember my name?" the bald guy asks as he gazes out the window.

Liza remembers from when he first picked her up. "Joey," she says sadly.

Joey nods while looking through the window. "And you're Liza."

"Yes," Liza says softly. The man's tone has lightened—there's still hope.

They both stare through the window in silence.

"You shouldn't have gotten in my van, Liza."

"I know," she sighs.

Joey tracks a lady with his eyes as she leaves the store. "How many people do you think have gotten in this van?"

Liza isn't sure how to answer. "A lot?"

Joey looks over at her. "That's not a number."

Liza can feel him looking at her and she doesn't like it. She keeps her eyes fixed on the window, fighting the urge to put her head down and close her eyes. If she can keep him talking to her, maybe he'll let her go. Or maybe the police will show up and rescue her. She just needs to keep from angering him.

"Um...five?" Liza replies.

Joey returns his gaze to the window. "Twenty-seven."

Liza catches her breath. She's fucked.

"And how many do you think have left this van alive?" He looks at her again.

Liza feels his stare. Tears well in her eyes as she struggles to stay focused on the window. "None," she says woefully.

Joey looks back through the window. A man exits the store and walks to his car, his shadow trailing far behind.

"When was the last time you watched the sunset, Liza?"

Liza notices that his tone has softened again. She needs to keep him like this.

"Hmm," Liza stalls while thinking of an answer. She matches his tone, "A long time ago. I can't really remember."

Joey gestures to the window, "You should watch this one then. It's your last."

Liza should be scared by his words, but his tone is relaxed and he's not actually harming her right now. She takes a chance by asking a question of her own.

"Is there anything I can do to leave here, Joey?" she asks softly.

Joey thinks for a moment before rising from his chair. "Watch the sunset," he says as he walks behind her.

Liza tenses up as Joey moves behind her, then relaxes as he continues on to the van's rear door. She watches him kneel beside the long black case she'd seen earlier. As he focuses on the case, Liza peeks at the knife on the other side of the chair. It's only a few feet away from her—so close—but there's nothing she can do with it. She looks back at Joey, fearful of whatever evil he's going to remove from the black case. Liza holds her breath.

A latch clicks open, followed by another latch. Joey raises the lid to reveal an electric bass guitar resting inside. Liza exhales in relief.

"My dad had one of those," Liza says to him.

Joey removes a packet of bass strings from the felt-lined case. "One of what?" he asks.

"A guitar," she says.

Joey clicks the case closed.

"Well, I mean a bass," she says.

Liza notices Joey snicker.

"He always corrected me and told me it's not a guitar—it's a bass."

Joey continues snickering as he walks back to his chair. Liza avoids eye contact but she knows she's making progress with him.

"How many strings did he play?" Joey asks quietly from the chair. He tears open the packet.

"Four," Liza says. She can tell from Joey's face that he's very interested in what she's saying. "He would sit me on his lap and make me count every string."

Liza reads the name on the packet of strings: DR Black Beauties. She doesn't recognize the name so she continues talking about her dad's bass collection.

"He had lots of basses. He tried teaching me to play one but it was too big for me."

Joey removes a coiled black string from the packet.

"He wouldn't let me touch his favorite one though."

Joey looks at her. She makes eye contact this time and notices that his eyes have softened.

"Which one was his favorite?" Joey asks.

"I think it was called a Rickenmacher or Rockenmacher, something like that."

Joey drops the packet to the floor and widens the loop in the coiled string. "Rickenbacker," he tells her.

"Yeah!" Liza says with quiet enthusiasm. She's connecting with him.

Joey places the coiled string over Liza's head. She fights the fear erupting in her gut as Joey works it down loosely around her neck.

"Isn't there another way, Joey?" she asks softly.

Joey's face darkens. He shakes his head slowly.

Liza's eyes well with tears. Hope is vanishing fast.

Joey sits in his chair and stares through the window. He puts a fresh cigarette between his lips, opens the Zippo cover and works the flint. A tall flame rises from the lighter. Joey leans his cigarette into the flame—it burns red and smoky. He snaps the lighter closed.

Liza has to try again. She musters a friendly voice, "My dad had one of those lighters."

Joey exhales a large cloud of smoke. He takes another drag from the cigarette and continues staring out the window.

Liza's comment didn't hit the mark. Fear quickly builds inside her.

"Do you see that little hill out there in the desert, Liza?"

Defeated and fearful, Liza doesn't care to look anywhere in particular. She nods to satisfy him.

"That's where I'm gonna bury you tonight. You'll be with Candy —I buried her there two months ago."

Liza's swallows her breath. Tears pour from her eyes.

Joey casually points to a man in the parking lot. "Look at that guy walking to his car, Liza."

Liza stops responding. Hands latched to her waist, ankles cuffed and a thick loop of metal wire around her neck, she's given up.

"That guy doesn't know you're in here. He's just right there— behind the glass—but he doesn't know."

Liza feels Joey look at her. She keeps her eyes locked on the window.

"Nobody knows, Liza."

Liza closes her eyes. "Please God help me," she says aloud.

Rolling paper crackles as Joey takes a deep drag from his cigarette. He butts it out in the wall ashtray and stands up.

"Open your eyes," Joey menaces.

Liza sobs and shakes her head. She feels a tap on her head, followed by the sound of a snapped finger in front of her. She opens her eyes.

Joey stands above her, staring darkly into her eyes. He slowly draws the curtain across the window.

Panic overwhelms Liza. "God please hel—"

Joey pounces on her, grabbing her throat and pushing her to the ground. She instinctively pulls at her hands to defend herself— the cuffs dig into her wrists.

"Say hi to your dad for me," Joey tells her.

Joey releases her throat and grabs the ends of the bass string as Liza gasps for air. She feels the noose tighten around her neck as he yanks the ends together and hastily ties a double knot. Her eyes bulge as her arteries constrict.

"Why is this happening to me?" she thinks.

The van's interior is awash in red light as Joey grabs her throat again and squeezes. Liza looks into his black eyes. He lifts his body up and leans forward, putting his full weight on her throat. Liza's vision dims.

"Come on girl, gimme your breath!" Joey says wildly.

Joey releases her throat and Liza gasps for air. He puts his mouth over hers and sucks.

"God, why is this happening!" she cries inside.

Joey sits up and straddles Liza's chest as she gasps for air. The noose has made her groggy but she's still conscious. Again Joey grabs her throat, lifting his body up and placing his full weight on her. Liza stomps her heels against the carpeted floor. Her eyes feel like they're popping out of her head.

Liza sees Joey's white hair jutting out wildly from the sides of his head. His demon eyes are full of life.

"Come on bitch I want your breath!"

Liza's vision dims further. Joey returns to straddling her but continues gripping her throat tightly as he puts his mouth over hers and sucks.

"Why God?" Liza wonders. She loses consciousness.

With his mouth over hers, Joey releases Liza's throat. She unconsciously gasps—a loud sucking noise fills the van as he pulls off her and sits up. Joey wipes his mouth as Liza clings to life.

From her bed, Liza sees her father standing above her, a bass guitar strapped over his shoulder.

"Hi daddy!" Liza says excitedly.

Liza's father ignores her.

"Daddy, don't you know me?" she asks.

Her father suddenly slaps her across the face, "Wake up bitch!"

Liza wakes up. She's confused and she can barely see. She knows she's in a red room, there's a bald guy above her and she's very uncomfortable.

"Wake up bitch, I want one more!"

She feels the bald guy squeeze her throat.

"You're gonna die now girl!"

She senses his body rise above her as the pressure on her throat increases. Her vision goes dark.

"Gimme that breath!" she hears in the darkness. Something wet sucks on her mouth.

Liza hears no more.

Epilogue

You used to be so nice to me. I'd hear from you at least once a day —the words you'd whisper to me were loving and kind. Throughout the day, you'd tell everyone you met how much I meant to you. The music you played at work kept me in mind all day long. At night, before bed, you'd kneel in humility. You devoted yourself to me for years—decades even. And all along the way, I was there.

Then you went and ruined it.

Time and again, you violated my rules. You idolized man, exalting him and worshiping his gold. You treated others like animals, blind to the fact that you are an animal, too. You trashed the world—my world—out of selfishness and spite. You flaunted your pitiful wealth while children starved. You knew they starved —you laughed at their suffering. You ate from a trough of lies and beckoned others to join you. You spat venom at widows and orphans. You brought harm to the world I created.

One man saved you, now one man destroys you. You've lost control of yourself and you've lost control of the world I made for you. A new chapter is unveiled in which you and your brethren are excluded. Today, you perish. Tomorrow doesn't exist. You will never wake again. Good riddance.

Freewheelin' with Ron Johnson

Note: The following interview contains minor spoilers for *Televangelist* and major spoilers for *Lunch Special*. Interview conducted June 21, 2018 with a pre-publication release of *Lunch Special*. Used by permission of *Indie Author Coterie*.

When Ron Johnson agreed to meet me at a diner off Boulder's main highway, he told me to "look for the long-haired guy wearing a Black Sabbath shirt". Upon my arrival, I realized that a description was unnecessary because Ron Johnson sticks out in a crowd. Wild hair riding atop a tall frame certainly sets him apart, but what most caught my eye is the restlessness—Johnson is a man in constant motion. That constant motion translated through to our interview, where Ron's manic energy steamrolled my prepared questions and turned our brief interview into something else entirely.

I see you're a Black Sabbath fan.

JOHNSON: [laughs] Yeah, I love Sabbath. My wife and I saw them twice at the Hollywood Bowl. Best concert I've ever been to—they ended it with a big fuckin' fireworks show.

Funny, my friend saw them and also mentioned the fireworks. Do you attend a lot of concerts?

JOHNSON: I don't how many is a lot but I do try and see bands that matter to me when they come around. In the past few years I've seen The Cure, Depeche Mode, The Cult, A-ha, Rush, Motley Crue, Jane's Addiction, and a lot more I'm forgetting. I'm pretty much playing catch up for a lifetime of missed music, I mean I'd never even been to a concert prior to 2007.

Seriously?

JOHNSON: Yeah. I never had any money growing up which lead to me being a very cheap adult, but after I got married my wife was able to get me out to a concert for the first time: Genesis at the Hollywood Bowl. I distinctly remember two things about that show: the huge CGI man on the screen behind the band during *In The Cage*, and middle-aged people in the audience smoking weed.

Sounds like a party.

JOHNSON: [laughs] For them maybe but not for me. I had a security clearance through my aerospace job that I took very seriously. I was very by-the-book back then and just way too serious about life in general. So when I saw these middle-aged guys smoking joints in the crowd, enjoying their lives and not giving a shit about how it might affect their jobs, it really opened my eyes. I figured, "If they can do it, why can't I?"

And you were, what, early-thirties at the time?

JOHNSON: Something like that. And it's not like I hadn't smoked weed before, I smoked a lot of weed back in high school. But I hadn't smoked after I went in the Army and I toed the line all the way into my working career. And honestly it wasn't really about wanting to smoke weed, it was more about having the freedom to do whatever I wanted when I wasn't at work. It was a question of whether I wanted my employer to control my personal life.

And the answer was?

JOHNSON: Well, I mean look at me? If I don't scream stoner, I don't know what does.

Now that you mention it…

JOHNSON: I do want to say though, I'm not really that much of a stoner. I smoke weed whenever the mood hits me, usually if I'm watching something good on TV or if I'm listening to music, but that's probably once a week or so and only at night.

Ah…like a stoner?

JOHNSON: [laughs] Yeah I guess. I just feel that if I'm going to label myself as something, I need to live up to it. I'm a lightweight with the weed and I don't need Tommy Chong or [Trailer Park Boys character] Ricky LaFleur challenging me to a bong-ripping contest.

So labels are important to you?

JOHNSON: I think if people are gonna call themselves something then they need to go forward with it full blast. For instance,

I'm wearing my Sabbath shirt but I had this moment of hesitation when I told you that I'm a fan because the fact is that I haven't heard all of their albums. I've heard all the Ozzy ones and a Dio one and I love those. But I don't wanna get called out as a poser or something by some real hardcore fans. There's a lot of posers in the world nowadays and I ain't trying to be another one.

That's still more albums than most people would know though.

JOHNSON: Right right, it's just a weird thing I have. There are very few things that I'm comfortable saying that I *am* because of that legitimacy thing.

Okay, so then what are you?

JOHNSON: Well, I'm a music fan first and foremost, and within music I can say that I'm a big Rush fan and a certifiable kook for XTC.

I'm familiar with Rush but what is XTC?

JOHNSON: It's probably best not to get me started on XTC because I won't stop, so I'll just say a little about them. They're an English band from the seventies-eighties-nineties with brilliant music that never got played on the radio. Long story short, I flew to a small town in England last year for an XTC band convention with a hundred other kooks and made friends with the coolest people I've ever met.

You flew there just for a concert?

JOHNSON: Nope, no concert, just a convention with other fans. The bassist and drummer made an appearance but the band has been broken up for many years now.

That's pretty intense.

JOHNSON: Yes, very intense. I can't explain why their music would drive me to a small town in England, but it did. It's like it dingles some kind of nerd bell in my head that results in huge amounts of auditory pleasure. That convention was an incredible experience and a highlight of my life for a variety of reasons.

Should I ask why?

JOHNSON: [laughs] Nah, let's just move on. If we talk XTC I'll never stop.

Okay, shall we discuss *Lunch Special*?

JOHNSON: Cool man, let's do it.

For starters, what is *Lunch Special*?

JOHNSON: *Lunch Special* is a collection of three increasingly dark short stories designed to bring a downer mood to the reader. My goal was to have people finish the book and feel the need to step outside for fresh air afterwards.

You mention that the stories are increasingly dark—so the order matters?

JOHNSON: Definitely. I sequenced the stories for the best trip, similar to what a band would do on an album side. Imagine listening to something like *Animals* by Pink Floyd or anything from Tangerine Dream—if you skip around instead of listening straight through you'll lose the energy that the artist intended. That's why I don't call *Lunch Special* a compilation, because it's not. The book is a bitter dose of medicine meant to be swallowed in a single, miserable gulp.

Having read the early release, I understand your point. Reading the stories out of order would disrupt the vibe.

JOHNSON: Exactly. Once a reader has opened my book, I try to do all I can to entertain them. That extends beyond the text, encompassing the cover art and in this case the pacing. Even the original five-story concept was laid out in a way to toy with the reader's mood.

Interesting, so the book was originally supposed to include five stories?

JOHNSON: Yep, three downers and two upbeat ones, plus a creepy host.

A host?

JOHNSON: Yeah. Remember the Crypt Keeper from *Creepshow*? I was trying something similar to that, where each story would be introduced by a clown named Cap'n Bonkers. He'd foreshadow the mood of the upcoming story by role-playing with balloon animals, then he'd eventually yell "Roll Tape" and the story would begin.

That's pretty odd.

JOHNSON: [laughs] Oh yeah, I loved it! I had two full intros written with Bonkers but I eventually had to pull the plug on him because it was just too confusing for the reader. Putting something that visual into print is very hard without a good explanation and I don't think my readers would be happy having to read a Bonkers instruction manual as a prerequisite for *Lunch Special*. I politely asked Cap'n Bonkers to leave and off he went.

Did that impact any of the stories?

JOHNSON: No, the stories all stood on their own without him, he was just an emcee who would ratchet up the mood. Clowns are inherently off-putting and even a positive story would be tense for the reader if it was first introduced by Cap'n Bonkers. They'd be waiting for that creepy fucker to pop out of a box at some point.

So then what did you do with the other two stories?

JOHNSON: The other two stories just never got written. I have parts of them done and know the basic outline but after writing the downers that appear in *Lunch Special* I wasn't in the mood to attempt two more with a completely different flavor. If I'm going to add an upbeat story to the book, it would have to be two upbeat stories to keep the pacing symmetrical.

What do you mean by symmetrical?

JOHNSON: Let me try to explain. The three stories in *Lunch Special* are all downers which present a consistent mood, right? Now, if I add a fourth story to the mix that has an entirely different mood from the other three, where would I put it? It can't fit anywhere without being an oddball. But if I added two stories to the mix—fives stories total—I can fit the two oddballs in as the second and fourth stories. I would then have a downer story followed by an upper, followed by another downer, and so on. That was my plan, to alternate the mood throughout the book like a little roller coaster, ultimately ending the ride in Joey's loving arms.

I see. Will those other two stories appear in a future book?

JOHNSON: They'll probably appear at some point. For now I just want to give my mind a rest from all the death and destruction.

Alright, I want to delve into each story but since we're here, let's discuss your writing process.

JOHNSON: Yeah sure.

First off, how do you create a story? Is it a brainstorming exercise, is it something that just occurs to you one day, or is it something else entirely?

JOHNSON: That's difficult to answer since I'm not always sure where my ideas come from, but I can say pretty confidently that it's not a brainstorming exercise. When I was writing *The [Jim Bakker] Foodbucket Fanpage*, that constant satirical approach would naturally lead to these little fictional inserts that I could use to drive my point home. I was also writing stoned for some of that stuff too, so that would have helped me branch out on those fictional tangents.

Would you say that cannabis plays a role for you in developing a story?

JOHNSON: As much as I'd like that to be true, I think it's more accurate to say that cannabis helps me enhance existing stories rather than create them from scratch.

I see. Moving on from your blog, how did you arrive at the ideas for your two books?

JOHNSON: The concept for *Televangelist* came to me after seeing my blog profiled in a dissertation done by a Canadian dude getting his doctorate. This might sound strange, but seeing my old work after having not looked at it for years was like injecting rocket fuel into the creative areas of my brain. I literally went home that night and began writing a story.

Just like that?

JOHNSON: Yep. I didn't even have to think, I just sat down and my fingers started hacking away at the keys. It was really incredible how much poured out of me that first night.

And you just wrote the whole story out like that?

JOHNSON: I put down pieces of the story, maybe sixteen pages worth or so, and it was all out of order. I think the first thing to come was the healing scene where Bart is hammering away on the guy with back pain, and after that was the ending, and probably the Japan scene after that.

Ah, so you didn't start writing from page one?

JOHNSON: Nope, I very rarely conceive of a story from the beginning. One thing that's pretty consistent for me is that I always know the ending to my stories, or something approximating the end, before I know how the stories begin. If I didn't know the end, I'd have no goal to work towards.

Interesting. Is that the same way you approached *Lunch Special***?**

JOHNSON: Yep. I knew the ending of "For Dog and Country" from the start, in fact I knew the very last line in the story. "Murder, American Style" went through two incarnations, both of which I knew the ending to. "Joey" is an offshoot but I obviously knew that Liza wasn't gonna make it in the end.

Let's talk about those stories, starting with "For Dog and Country." Along the same topic, where did you get the idea for this story?

JOHNSON: [laughs] Well I'm sure I'll sound like a lunatic here, but this one came to mind after I had an argument with a neighborhood guy and his wife about my dog.

Okay, go on.

JOHNSON: I had my old twenty-pound terrier out on our nightly walk and we came up to this lady who was walking her young Labrador. Our dogs got in a minor scuffle and the lady freaked out and took him to the vet for emergency treatment. The vet proceeded to ream her up the ass on the bill, and the lady sent her husband to my door demanding payment.

Was the other dog okay?

JOHNSON: Yeah he was fine, but once this dipshit shows up at the emergency room they're gonna find something to get paid for even if her dog doesn't need it. Let me say that I'm a real polite guy and I'm fair about things. I was sympathetic to her dog because my crafty old guy did get the better of him and I could see he was shaken up, but he wasn't hurt. I mean if he was actually hurt, I'd take him to the vet myself. It's no secret that I love dogs.

Was her husband with her at the time?

JOHNSON: No, and it's too bad he wasn't because he could have kept her under control for what came next. I'm standing there apologizing to her and she begins very rudely asking for my phone number and address. I could have just told her to fuck off but like I said I'm a polite guy and I was willing to help with any vet bill even though I didn't see a reason for one. So I accepted her rudeness, I gave her my info, and then she decided to wag her finger in my face and tell me I'd be "hearing from her."

Uh-oh.

JOHNSON: [laughs] Uh-oh is right. Be rude all you want but don't be wagging no fucking fingers in my face.

And then?

JOHNSON: A couple days later I get a thing in the mail from animal control saying that my dog was reported as a vicious dog and I had to fill out these statements about the incident. You can imagine how much that pissed me off because it's quite frankly not true. So I spend a day gathering evidence to show that my dog isn't vicious and this woman is full of shit. The next day she sends her husband to my door with a vet bill. I told him that I was open to helping with the bill up until the point that his wife wagged her finger in my face and put my dog on paper with the city. After a long discussion, I eventually agreed to pay half of the bill to be neighborly but the guy *refused*. The fucking guy tells me he'll see me in court and leaves.

Was that when you decided it was time to burn them to death?

JOHNSON: [laughs] Nah man, if it was just that I'd still be sane about it, but it got worse. Consider that this guy and his wife live two streets away from me, so a normal dog-walking route wouldn't bring them by my house. And yet, lo and behold, here comes his fucking wife walking her dog by my house every night. And, lo and behold, every morning I'm finding dog shit on the sidewalk in front of my house.

Uh-oh.

JOHNSON: [laughs] Goddamn right uh-oh! Now I'm being actively provoked and I'm considering my options.

Was one of those options burning them to death with gasoline?

JOHNSON: [laughs] Not quite, but you can imagine that the thoughts going through my head weren't, uh, pure.

Did he ever take you to court?

JOHNSON: Nah fuck no, he had nothing to go to court with. Our little dogs had a little fight, big deal.

Did the dog poop ever stop?

JOHNSON: Oh yeah. I started making appearances outside my house when they'd walk by to get the message across that I'm not a guy they should fuck with.

You should send them a copy of your book.

JOHNSON: [laughs] Don't think the thought hasn't crossed my mind!

Alright so moving forward into story development, how did you turn that experience into "For Dog and Country"? The plot is pretty far removed from a simple neighborhood spat.

JOHNSON: Anger and frustration sends my creativity into overdrive and after that incident I was thinking a lot about what the punishment should be for people who fuck with other peoples' dogs. That quickly evolved into the actual ending of the story, and from there I would jot down notes as different parts of the story revealed itself to me. I have a notebook filled with all kinds of notes, everything from character backgrounds to scene descriptions to one-liners.

How much of the story was developed through that method?

JOHNSON: Hmm, maybe seventy percent or so. It's hard to say because my notes are always such a jumble of framework and content.

And this is all before you sit down to write?

JOHNSON: Yep. I toy around like that for months before I ever write something. I'm basically laying out all the milestones I need to hit in order to reach the finish line so that when I actually sit down to write, all I have to do is connect the dots.

Can you give an idea of something in the story that wasn't planned out that way?

JOHNSON: Off the top of my head, the Joey encounter at 7-Eleven and the part where Dave has his PTSD flashback.

Interesting.   What inspired you to write those unplanned scenes?

JOHNSON: Well for Joey, I always loved his character in *Televangelist* and I thought it'd be cool to bring him into the story as an inside joke to people who read that book. And honestly, when I was a kid I always thought it was the coolest thing when characters from one show made a guest appearance on a different show. So Joey made a guest appearance which led to him getting his own chapter, too.

He got a spin-off show!

JOHNSON: [laughs] Yeah pretty much.

And the PTSD scene with Dave, what inspired that?

JOHNSON: I think that grew from injecting myself into the story and imagining Dave's mental state as he's heading down the freeway to take these people out. I'm very proud of that scene—it was difficult to write but I think it does a great job of informing the reader as to what's going on with Dave. As it turned out, it's also very important to the story.

Right, this is the scene where we learn just how unstable Dave really is.

JOHNSON: Yep. Here's a man stricken with terrible feelings of guilt and fear, who can in a split-second turn off those emotions and kill a man with his bare hands. I also like what I did with Lupe in this scene. Even after witnessing Dave freaking out, she still reaches out to him and reassures him that everything will be alright. She lets him know that he's not alone.

I thought it would be an interesting romance until you pulled the plug on it.

JOHNSON: [laughing] I love it! I believe the final line in that scene was "they move forward together." Or not.

Regarding that, did you always plan for Dave to commit suicide?

JOHNSON: Yeah, it had to be that way. The only thing Dave cared about in the entire world was Bobby. Once Bobby was gone, there was nothing left for him to live for. Sorry Lupe. By the way, when the book included the Cap'n Bonkers intros he actually laughs at Lupe's plight as the last person left.

Well that's just *mean*.

JOHNSON: [laughs] Indeed it was. Cap'n Bonkers took things to another level.

Let's go through the same questions with "Murder, American Style." How did the story develop?

JOHNSON: The original idea for "Murder, American Style" came out of my frustration with the fucking gun kooks after that guy in Vegas shot everyone from his hotel room. I remember seeing all these dumb fucks spouting their usual NRA-programmed nonsense and I decided to write something to vent my frustration. I suppose I could have just bought an assault rifle instead and gone on a murderous rampage at a gun rally, but that's not my style.

Better to have your characters do that, huh?

JOHNSON: Exactly, I can just lob rounds in with a pen and paper. And that's what I did at first, although the story changed entirely from where it began.

How so?

JOHNSON: The first thing I wrote was this real killer Cap'n Bonkers intro where he mows down a bunch of balloons with an assault rifle. That led to me drawing up a chilling little story called "Murder Diary" which was essentially a log kept by a guy who'd decided he wanted to spend his forties ridding the world of shitheads. The character would explain all the things that go into executing a murder—the clothes, the weapon, when to strike, all these little details. I thought it was a little too close to *Taxi Driver* but it was kinda fun to think about so I kept it alive. I had some issues with figuring out how to make the logic work and once I was actually faced with writing it, the whole thing changed drastically.

Considering that "Murder, American Style" is nothing like what you're describing, that must have been a very drastic change.

JOHNSON: Oh yeah and it happened quick, like within a couple days. I took a few days off after completing "For Dog and Country" but mentally I was preoccupied with "Murder, American Style" since I knew I'd have to start writing it. I ended up having a dream one night that gave me the gun rally idea and I decided to make that the new ending.

A dream, really?

JOHNSON: It was more like that state you're in right before you fall asleep and when you first wake up, when you're sort of drifting in and out of consciousness. Those times tend to be pretty rewarding creatively and that's how I figured out the gun rally angle.

Did the new ending require you to change anything with the main story?

JOHNSON: [laughs] Yeah I threw the whole thing out!

Seriously?

JOHNSON: Yeah, I spent a few hours slogging through a couple pages of the story and realized there was no way I could make the beginning reach the new ending I envisioned, it just wasn't gonna happen. I took a break, went outside and asked myself, "How would a story with that new ending begin?" When I sat back down, I started writing it just how you see it except the guy was in a Walmart.

Did you use any of the original material for the new story?

JOHNSON: Nope, it all went into the archives for a later date. There's some good lines in the original stuff but I'm far more pleased with what "Murder, American Style" became. I love launching volleys at racists and the fucking gun kooks.

You might want to be careful with people like that, eh?

JOHNSON: You know what, here's what the gun kooks don't understand: I have a gun, too. They assume that people who're opposed to their gun-lovin' insanity are all pacifist hippies who want to fix the world's problems with flower power but in reality most gun owners aren't part of the fucking gun cult. Imagine that.

Let me play devil's advocate and argue that the "gun kooks" as you call them are actually fighting to protect the Second Amendment and your right to own a gun.

JOHNSON: That tired old gun rights line is bullshit because nobody is taking anyone's guns away. The kooks buy into this garbage and think they're doing something for America but it's all nonsense. They've had the NRA convince them that gun ownership is patriotic and yet how many of them are veterans? How about you go sacrifice a few years of your life serving your country before you come spouting off about how patriotic you are. Take that flag you're wrapping yourself in and set fire to it along with yourself because you're counterfeit. Phony-fucking-patriots these people.

That's reminiscent of the opening scene in "Murder, American Style" when Johnny buys flag-print clothing to blend in with the horde.

JOHNSON: [laughs] Yeah, he needs to wrap himself in the flag to fit in with the rest of the so-called patriots.

He even bought a Second Amendment belt buckle, right?

JOHNSON: Classiest part of the outfit!

So it's safe to say that you're a gun owner who supports limits on gun ownership?

JOHNSON: Yeah, but think how ludicrous it sounds even asking that? Guns are made to kill, why the fuck wouldn't we control them? That doesn't mean they aren't cool. The design, the craftsmanship, the power—all of that is really attractive. But it's pretty much common sense that people shouldn't be allowed to buy assault rifles. Why the fuck would you need an assault rifle? To hunt? I can hunt with a flamethrower, in fact I can hunt and cook at the same time. Should we all be allowed to own flamethrowers? How about a goddamn tank, I can hunt with that too. And the extended magazine, let me say that if you need an extended mag for hunting then you should lose your hunting license because you obviously can't shoot for shit. The baloney heads who support all this shit are just repeating whatever the fucking NRA tells them, and you know what else? They're fucking racists too, so fuck 'em.

Which brings me to my next topic: the racial undertones contained in "Murder, American Style."

JOHNSON: [laughs] Oh it ain't an undertone, it's an overtone.

I'll admit I was shocked at how explicit it was.

JOHNSON: Yeah well you know what, if you're at a goddamn *Open Carry* gun rally then you're most likely dropping the n-word and everything else on the regular. These are grown men who're so scared of other people that they pay to be part of a club that fights for their so-called right to carry a gun with them everywhere they go. Call it a hunch, but I'm gonna say that the people they're scared of aren't the people they interact with every day in their little corner of *Whitesville*.

Would you say they might be scared of an African-American cowboy?

JOHNSON: Ah, the black cowboy. I hope my readers were able to put their hang-ups aside and laugh when he first appeared, because it was obvious to me the moment I wrote it that the man was doomed. He's the token black guy who's been put on stage so the whole crowd can pretend that they aren't racists. Meanwhile, he's forced to stand apart from the other cowboys and of course he's the first person to die when the horde is looking for a target. It illustrates the hypocrisy of all these people. Without the black cowboy it's basically a Klan rally. Add him to the stage and voila —we're not the Klan no more!

Considering how openly you used a word that has been banned from literary existence, did you have any concern about offending people or facing backlash?

JOHNSON: I'm aware that seeing the n-word in print might put some people off, but racism is ugly and sugarcoating things is a juvenile way to deal with reality. As for offending people, I don't give a shit if white people take offense but I would feel bad if black people or any other group fingered by the story's racists were offended. I can say that my intentions are pure, but there are cultural blind spots that I as a white guy might be missing.

I guess a good way to say it is that I tried to do right, even if it came out wrong. I don't think it came wrong though. I think it came out just right.

It's interesting that you aren't worried about offending white people, only minorities?

JOHNSON: [laughs] Yeah, of course. The country is way too politically correct today so I fully expect white people to be offended on behalf of black people, all while the message of the story flies right over their heads. People need to take a chill pill and stop trying to stifle every little thing that makes them uncomfortable. I mean, I'm a white guy who's outing racists and exposing the evils of the gun lobby in one fell swoop. I'm on your team, dummies.

The conclusion of the story alludes to Johnny killing his mother before going on a shooting rampage at his high school. Let's discuss that.

JOHNSON: Welcome to Texas!

What do you mean by that?

JOHNSON: Texas residents can buy an assault rifle once they're eighteen years old. There's no background check, no licensing requirement and no waiting period. Being mentally ill doesn't matter unless you self-report yourself. The events I describe can happen tomorrow, and the next day, and the next day.

Ah, is that really true?

JOHNSON: Yep. Nice place, huh?

Maybe the new slogan should be "Texas: Remember to take your pill."

JOHNSON: [laughs] Oh let me tell you something cool, remember the Australian band Men at Work?

They had a few hits right? *Land Down Under* **and another one?**

JOHNSON: Yeah, they're a killer band if you've never heard their albums. Anyways, the character name Johnny Jyde is a combination of two of their songs: *Be Good Johnny* and *Dr Hekyll and Mr Jyde*. I thought that fit remarkably well in a story about a kid hearing voices in his head.

Is that something you've done before?

JOHNSON: This is the first time I've used a music reference for a character's name but I've referenced music stuff before. You might have caught the voice in Johnny's head telling him to "kill 'em all" which is the title of a Metallica album. *Televangelist* had a chapter titled "Master & Servant" which is the name of a Depeche Mode song.

So it seems you like to sprinkle these things throughout your writing?

JOHNSON: I love putting little Easter eggs in the things I write. *Televangelist* even had a cameo appearance by someone who looked a lot like [Depeche Mode frontman] Dave Gahan.

Really, where?

JOHNSON: It's in that same "Master & Servant" chapter. He's the vacationing healer named English Dave.

I'll have to look at that again.

JOHNSON: Dave would make a great televangelist if the music thing doesn't work out.

Are there others you haven't mentioned?

JOHNSON: Oh yeah there's a ton of stuff like that. If we're talking *Televangelist* I'll tell you right off the bat that the story begins at 4:20pm which is stoner code for gettin' high. The [Canadian comedy trio] Trailer Park Boys are referenced in the healing chapter. I mentioned Bart being "big in Japan" which is an Alphaville song, and chapter titles like "Goodbye" and "Master & Servant" have multiple interpretations. There's also things like the homeless guy being Jesus, gum being an omen, and the dimensions of Bart's office being multiples of six. It's very fun to do things like that when I'm writing.

And in *Lunch Special*?

JOHNSON: The story isn't as broad but I can think of a few. The name of Dave's pest control company, "Eleven-Bravo Pest Exterminators," is an inside reference to the Army job code for infantry, who themselves could be called pest exterminators. Gum shows up as an omen again with Jake and Emily, as does the triple-six when Jake's in the convenience store. And the appearances of both Bart and Joey are Easter eggs for readers of *Televangelist*.

Ah, Joey. Shall we talk about him now?

JOHNSON: Sure. I love Joey even though the story was a little too extreme for my taste.

Really?

JOHNSON: Yeah, you gotta consider that I have to inhabit my characters in order to speak like them. So as I'm writing about Joey, I'm forced to imagine what he would say and do with the girl and it felt really gross. The guy is mentally tormenting her, telling her she's going to die and showing her where he's going to bury her. Then he sucks on the girl's mouth as he's strangling her. After I was done I felt like I should call the cops on myself.

I'd say it was pretty tame compared to other stories I've read.

JOHNSON: I would agree, I mean Joey could've sawed her head off if I wanted him too and that would be pretty wild for the reader. I didn't think that was his style though. The guy's a bass player so I thought he'd prefer hands-on work that keeps his hands in shape while protecting them from cuts. If he was just cutting off heads that'd be easy for me to write.

Why is that?

JOHNSON: I'm not exactly sure, maybe because it seems more cartoonish to me. The way Joey does it seems crueler. If he sawed off her head or gouged her eyes or something, big deal. But the intimacy of Joey's morbid chat, the strangling and sucking on her mouth, that was difficult to write.

I did find the sucking part strange.

JOHNSON: That was a Ted Bundy thing, he would make a point of breathing in his victims' last breath.

Really? I didn't know that.

JOHNSON: Yeah. I've always been interested in serial killers and that Bundy factoid always stuck with me. Serial killers are fascinating people. I'm not trying to glorify them or anything but the kind of brain that comes up with that kinda shit is not one that I possess. I'd give him a solid ten points for originality but zero points on the execution.

Zing!

JOHNSON: Seriously though, how many people can think that way? Did you know Bundy would lure victims by wearing a fake cast on his leg and asking women to help him load stuff in his car? And this other guy, I forget his name, but he would drug women and then wake them up with an audiotape of him telling them how fucked they were to be captured by him. It's so depraved as to defy logic, at least in my view.

Joey does something similar with Liza, right? He tells her she shouldn't have entered his van and that she's going to die.

JOHNSON: Hmm, you're right. What the fuck is wrong with me?

Do you also drive a van?

JOHNSON: No, but I love vans. Doesn't everybody?

Everyone except Liza.

JOHNSON: [laughs] Yeah, poor Liza. I found the chat that Joey had with her very morbid. What he's saying doesn't just apply to Liza, it applies to all of us. When death comes knocking, you're done. There ain't no escape, no magic potion you can drink to make it go away. Better enjoy the sunset while you can.

I noticed in your bio that you're an atheist. That strikes me as a very atheistic way of looking at the world.

JOHNSON: That's just the way the world works man. Regardless of what people wish and hope for, the reality is we're all going down and we're going down hard.

Have you always been an atheist?

JOHNSON: No, I actually grew up surrounded by Christians because members of my family ran a church. We were Pentecostals, those are the ones who flabber their tongues around during church like lunatics. I accepted Jesus Christ as my Lord and Savior on three different occasions but I don't think it ever took.

What made you leave?

JOHNSON: For one thing I was never feeling the whole tongue-talkin' shit. You were supposed to let the Holy Spirit flow through you. Well, I tried and nothing happened. I just stood there looking at all these other dipshits flabbing their tongues and wondering why it wasn't working for me.

You just didn't have enough faith, Brother Ron!

JOHNSON: Maybe. But I just found it very suspicious that these people who claimed that the Holy Spirit was speaking through them only had that happen on Sundays between 10am and noon. I never heard any of them say they went out of control with that shit on a Tuesday night inside a crowded grocery store.

That's a good point!

JOHNSON: I saw what turds they were too. All kinds of shenanigans going on in that church, and look even today with these goddamn Evangelicals? With all the shitting on other people going on in this country, the Evangelicals should be the very first people protesting but nope, not only do they say nothing, they cheer it on! They've thrown Jesus in the trash can, stuck their heads up their asses and asked for the remote.

But Brother Ron, aren't you also shitting on racists and gun kooks?

JOHNSON: [laughs] They deserve it though.

In all seriousness though, wouldn't you consider that hypocritical?

JOHNSON: No, because as an atheist I don't claim to be speaking for God. The Evangelicals sit there and protest abortion clinics, but guess what—they're getting abortions. They get all riled up about birth control and sex education in school but the truth is they're all fucking around in church and blowing each other left and right. Now—today—they're all tied up with the fucking adulterers, racists and con men in the Republican party, and they keep voting for them. What would Jesus think about that you fucking hypocritical assholes?

I take it you're a Democrat?

JOHNSON: Nah I'm an independent, I don't choose sides. Aligning with one or the other just allows them to craft a message to say exactly what I want to hear. I don't want them to tell me what I *want* to hear, I want them to tell me *what they think*. I want my leaders to have some goddamn conviction. Even if I disagree with them on certain issues, if they believe what they say and actually follow their own rules, that goes a long way with me.

Would you vote for a Christian candidate?

JOHNSON: How Christian?

I didn't know there were degrees of Christianity?

JOHNSON [laughs] Oh there are definitely levels to it. If you mean Christian like Jimmy Carter, sure I'd vote for him every day of the week. But if you mean Christian like [Former Arkansas Governor] Mike Huckabee, fuck no. Never.

What's wrong with Huckabee?

JOHNSON: The guy's a fake Christian who traded his bible for a MAGA hat. You can't support Donald Trump and be a Christian, it's impossible. It sucks too because the guy is a bass player. I'll look the other way on a lot of shit for a fellow bass player, but the guy is just too much with his hypocrisy and hell-spawn daughter. I'd vote for a bass-playing murderer over a bass-playing Mike Huckabee.

A bass-playing murderer...like Joey?

JOHNSON: Hey, Joey has conviction! You know what you're getting with him every time. The Huckster, on the other hand, appears to change with the wind, and the wind today is blowing from a giant fart somebody ripped in the White House.

Shall we talk about the White House farter?

JOHNSON: The guy gives me a headache. Can I just say a few things and move on?

Sure.

JOHNSON: Alright. I didn't vote for Trump but he won the election and I gave him a fair shot. He took his shot, he failed terribly and he continues to fail. I'm willing to overlook a lot of policy things because he did, after all, win the election, but I can't ignore shit that he intentionally wrecks and I can't ignore illegal behavior. The guy is breaking ethics laws all over the place, first and foremost by using his position to enrich himself and his family. He blatantly lies about anything and everything and he's intentionally fucking around with all the investigations swirling around him. On top of that, he's appointed goons to wreck nearly every cabinet position. And that's totally ignoring all the thugs surrounding him who've been convicted of crimes. Now he's pressing forward with the Space Force. Let me say that the first person launched into orbit by the Space Force needs to be one Donald J. Trump. "Excuse me gentlemen, do you have this spacesuit in a 4X?"

I'll close with a final question: Do you plan on writing any more books?

JOHNSON: After *Televangelist*, I told myself no. It was too much work for too little reward. Less than a year later, the urge struck me again and here I am with *Lunch Special*. In that time I've grown more comfortable as a writer and I've learned that a book in hand is all the reward I really need. The way I experience the world results in lots of ideas popping into my head so I don't think I have much choice in the matter. Another book is inevitable.

Thanks for your time, Ron.

JOHNSON: My pleasure.

Cap'n Bonkers Demo

The original concept for *Lunch Special* included a surreal host character, a clown named Cap'n Bonkers, who would introduce each story by interacting with balloon animals. His interaction with those balloons would paint the mood of the story and occasionally include details which would make sense only after the story was read. Weird, right? I ultimately axed the idea because it was too difficult to implement, but I felt that readers would enjoy seeing the other ideas I had brewing during production of *Lunch Special*.

Below, Cap'n Bonkers introduces "For Dog and Country" in the only intro that was formally completed. See if you can decipher the meaning.

* * *

A black table sits at the center of a shadowless, borderless white void. On the table, a stovepipe hat rests on its side, *Property Of Cap'n Bonkers* embroidered inside. A red foam nose sits next to the hat.

A cotton-gloved hand squeezes the corners of a tiny Ziploc bag to prop it open before pouring its powdery contents out on the table. The hand produces a playing card—the Joker—and draws the powder into one long, narrow line. A head full of bright red hair leans down to the table and traces the line with one loud snort.

Cap'n Bonkers leans back in his chair and coughs.

"Are we ready?" he asks the void.

Silence.

"I said are we fucking ready!?" he growls.

An impartial voice clicks in over an intercom, "Dave said two minutes."

"No we're ready now," Bonkers scowls into the void above him. "Tell him we're ready now."

Bonkers grabs the foam nose from the table and puts it back in place. "Goddamn movie stars," he grumbles under his breath.

The intercom clicks on again, "He's ready."

Bonkers pumps his arm. He dons the top hat and stands up. The table vanishes, leaving only Bonkers in the void. He smiles broadly and raises his index finger—watch this.

The clown curves his fingers to make a claw with each hand and turns them toward each other. Bonkers concentrates on his hands as he slowly brings them closer to each other. The fingertips touch. Bonkers looks at us and winks.

Clown hands blur together. Twisting, squeezing, pulling, they manipulate an object unknown to us. Bonkers stares into his hands as they whiz around. Faster and faster they move. His eyes strain red as he focuses on his handiwork. From within his twirling hands, a dim glow appears. A hum fills the void.

Bonkers suddenly throws his hands to the sides—all becomes still in the void. Five exquisite balloon creatures stand next to him. Four humans—two blue and two pink—and a blue dog.

Bonkers digs deeply into his pant pockets. His eyes wander as he searches.

"Found it," he says excitedly.

Bonkers raises the object to his face for inspection. The sharp end of a nail protrudes upward from his thumb and forefinger. The clown grins as his eyes betray mischief.

Nail in hand, Bonkers walks over to the balloon dog and pops it. Three other balloons spontaneously pop. Only one balloon remains: a pink one.

Bonkers looks at the last balloon and bursts into a laughing fit. Blue and pink rubber fragments, the remnants of the popped balloons, surround the lonely balloon.

Bonkers halts his laughter and slowly brings the nail close to the last balloon. Closer and closer the nail approaches. A half inch. A quarter inch. The balloon's delicate rubber skin prepares to kiss the nail's sharp end.

Bonkers changes course and hurls the nail into the void. The balloon survives.

"Wahh!" he taunts the balloon, twisting his fists around his eyes in a crying motion. A sad kazoo plays from the void.

"Roll it!" Cap'n Bonkers yells to the void.

A projector whirs into action. The void goes black.

More from Ron Johnson

Fiction–

Televangelist

Satire/Commentary–

The Jim Bakker Foodbucket Fanpage

(found at www.JimBakker666.blogspot.com)

About the Author

Ron Johnson is the creator of the satirical blog *The Jim Bakker Foodbucket Fanpage* and the author of *Televangelist*. A native of Long Beach, California, Ron currently resides in Colorado with his wife and dog.

When not busy writing, Ron enjoys listening to music and organic gardening.

Transitioner

It all began with a small, dusty hole in the ground. That small hole became a larger hole, then expanded further until it reached six, maybe seven-feet deep. Boy oh boy, I loved that level. Some soils become hard and clay-like that far down, but not there. The soil there was moist and smelled wonderfully rich and familiar. You'd never think it, but life thrived down there in the form of earthworms and a beautiful fabric-like network of roots. Everywhere you moved, roots existed. Those roots were life. But I kept going down. You have to keep going down, otherwise you'll get stuck there forever and become eternity's pin-headed doorman.

So down I went. Darkness fell as I descended towards the heat. Distant machinery chugged as I dug deeper. My dark world squeezed tight around me, compressing me and giving a sense of claustrophobia. But those feelings—phobias—are never too strong nowadays. They exist only as faint memories, like faded pictures in candlelight. In the Darkness, they have been unlearned. Still, that level was my least favorite. It offered me nothing but swampy warmth and compaction, and I knew I could do better.

Further into the Darkness I went. The earth around me exuded oil, smelly and thick. It coated me, lubricated me, as I twisted and writhed into the deep. Sound energy vibrated my earthen cocoon as the distant machinery drew closer. At this level I felt the temperature increase substantially, perhaps ten-fold. But that was fine. Pain doesn't exist in the Darkness. Neither does fear, for that matter.

The next level was difficult. Rocky, hot, loud and arduous, yet not without its joys. It was here that I felt tested, challenged. Without challenge or curiosity, the Darkness will become dull and monotonous. Some might prefer that—pin-headed door-men most certainly do. I do not. This level, then, made the Darkness fresh. I ground myself into the rock. I corkscrewed into it, grinding and grinding and grinding some more. Time isn't measured in the Darkness but in daylight terms my grinding efforts surely lasted months or even years. I entered the rock. I tasted the heat. I heard the machinery. I met the challenge and eventually the rock began to soften. Deeper still I went, grinding the rock away. Vibrations from the machine enveloped me as rock gave way to liquid. I squirmed into the liquid, hot and thick. It vibrated around me, within me. The machine and I were one. In the Darkness, I felt everything. Inside, outside, around and beyond. The sensation was incredible.

Still I wanted more. There must be more. There's always more.

I focused myself and disconnected from the machine. There is no animosity in the Darkness—the machine does not feel. In the liquid, hot and thick, I maneuvered myself towards the bottom where I understood it to be. Through the vibrating sludge, I encountered new rock. Different rock—porous rock. I began my grind. In an instant, the rock shattered inward and I was sucked inside.

Down I went. Inside the rock I fell, further and further. No fear, no pain, only wild curiosity at the promise the Darkness now presented to me. Vibrations from the machine quickly vanished as I fell further down into the rock. Soon, I sensed that I was no longer falling, but being pulled.

The falling motion ceased as vision suddenly awoke in my eyes. Worlds introduced themselves to me. Planets and stars shone in colors that shimmered and vibrated. They spoke to me; I spoke back. From the Darkness—through the Darkness—I found light. Indescribable light.

This present existence has no rules. I can return to the Darkness anytime. There is no pain—no fear—in the Darkness, but it offers no further challenge. My curiosity of it has been fulfilled. New worlds abound.